ADULT FICTION

Maya 29

Alice Joanou

Series editor: Maxim Jakubowski

MAYA 29

ISBN 1 85286 634 9

Series editor: Maxim Jakubowski

Published by Eros Plus
An imprint of Titan Books
42-44 Dolben Street
London SE1 0UP

First UK edition October 1995
1 3 5 7 9 10 8 6 4 2

British Library Cataloguing-in-Publication Data. A catalogue record for this book is available from the British Library.

Printed and bound in Great Britain by Cox and Wyman Ltd, Reading, Berkshire.

Contents

I

His Psychotic Scheherazade

She smelled like a metallic orgasm, and he was immediately seduced by the vague scent of her sickness. She gave it off like she was marking territory, and he knew the diagnosis before she opened her mouth. When he was in the presence of skillfully veiled illness the back of his neck tingled, and he felt a seizing up in his stomach that was always a struggle between arousal and fear. His psychiatric judgements weren't usually wrong, though he would never openly admit to professional diagnostics based upon a sensual reaction to patients.

His ethics were diminished when she walked into the office.

Her body was more perfume than flesh, her aroma natural and entirely deranged. It was a deep and subtle smell, and to a psychiatrist, the barbed labyrinth of a haunted body and hunted soul were the fundamental elements that would make the chase interesting.

Her lack of anxiety irritated him. She was as self-contained as an egg.

"I am Maya." Her voice was neutral, but he thought there was something in it that hinted at a muted scream. A pillowed cry.

"Good afternoon, Maya. I am Dr Lazar. I —"

"Maya 29."

"29?"

"The one before the 30th."

"I'm not quite sure I —"

"The 30th. The final Maya. The first and the last. She is the first and the last. She is my sister. My twin. My mother. My mouth to the centre."

She sat straight backed, on the edge of the leather chair as if teetering on the invisible tightrope she was walking between here and there. The there of insanity. She started to laugh and raised her gloved hand to cover her mouth, pressing the sound into her black leathered palm. Her laugh was grotesque; as if another creature appeared in the room. It left the instant she quieted. She kept her hand in front of her mouth for a moment longer. He waited.

"I don't mind that you hate my laugh," she said. He tried to hide his surprise but his brow moved too quickly to suppress.

"Most people do," she said.

"Maya, who recommended that you come see me?"

She smiled holding the secret in her mouth like a canary. "No one that you know. Not really."

She sat back and rested her head against the leather. Her black hair spread against the chair like an ink blot. He felt an erection hinting against the lining of his trousers and she smiled slightly as if she knew it. She unbuttoned her coat and he was a little disturbed by the hint of the red tattoo that peeked out of the edges of her dress. It looked as if it belonged to a greater whole that he could not see as it was obscured by her dress.

Her teeth were very white. Sharp. He found himself looking hard at her mouth. She smiled wider and he was surprised to see that her incisors were actually capped or possibly shaved into points. Fangs.

All the modern mechanisations of psychiatry were at his disposal, but he found himself avoiding its machinery. It was simple. He wanted to fuck her.

She was lovely, and he tried to make the usual categorisations to distract himself, but he was confused by her smell, confused by her presence; yet he was enjoying the strange twist she was casting on the day. He didn't want to listen to another tale of self-loathing, sexual compulsion or a hidden eating disorder. She was probably insane, possibly dangerous, and this pleased him. She hadn't done anything that gave him any overt realisation of her violence. It was intrinsic in her person. It was part of the scent she gave off.

"How can I help you?"

"You can't," she said.

Her head bent like a heavy flower on a weak stem. Delicate fingers moved in a stately crawl towards the hem of her skirt. There was sadness in the gesture of her hands and ordinarily this would have killed his desire, but her disease aroused him. When it looked as if she was going to pull her skirt up, she pushed it down. He followed the gesture of her hand and briefly glimpsed a black garter cutting a stark path through the middle of her white thigh. His eyes searched for the zenith of her body which was curtained by black silk. A powerful hole hidden by a very thin barrier of underclothing. Training forced him to shift his gaze. The eye-hooks of her boots ran up her calf and stared at him calmly. He wished to avoid her lips. Her gaze.

The arousal washed over him, warm and sticky as though blood was choking his neural network, drowning all logic. All the oaths and promises he had made to care for the sick were lost inside a deep thick red. He felt as if the electricity of his synapses was no longer carried in neural fluid, but that his thoughts and motor reactions were being delivered via a heavy stream of semen. Everything was slowing. Everything in the shrinking universe of his office was filtered through a singular desire. A lubricious warmth filled the consultation room — a heat that came from her cunt, her mouth, her eyes. Her body was emanating a scent that seemed to malnourish any medical responsibility he might have had towards her, and the queer lethargy rendered him helpless in front of her psychic nudity.

She waited.

Finally he spoke and the sound of his voice seemed to drift out of his mouth. "Why have you —"

"I wanted to. Come."

One corner of her mouth lifted ironically as if she were his accomplice rather than a prospective patient. He wondered if his guess at her condition was wrong, but instincts told him that he was in the presence of tangible danger and he wanted to linger in its sway. He wanted to stay inside the circle of her toxic presence longer than the professionally delineated forty-five minutes. Time did not seem to apply to her. He guessed at her age and thought she could have been anywhere between twenty and thirty.

Any will towards healing that he should have had was subsumed into the vortex of her black dress.

"I wanted to come before I vanish."

"Vanish?"

"Into the wound." She put her hand over the tattoo that cleaved her sternum. It had the shape and look of an injury.

"I want you to have my eulogy. I want you to deliver it."

"Maya, I'm afraid I am not following too clearly. You seem to think we have met before?"

"No. I've never met you. But I know…I know you'll take care of the eulogy."

"Are you ill?"

"I thought you were the judge of that."

She smiled. Deadpan grin. Not at him, but at his words. He felt he was incidental in her presence.

She stood, and waited for a moment by the chair. She studied him for a second and inside that instant it seemed she decided something. When she tilted her head, he was fascinated by the marvellously controlled strain of tendons against the white glassine stretch of her skin. His eyes drifted down her body and he was stricken by the lines of her breasts. The soft white flesh pushed up out of the black bodice, and the strange whisper of blue veins pushed over the hill of gland, tissue and nerve. He could see the suggestion of her nipples and her waist was pulled into a torturous V which gave way finally to a sigh of fleshy hip.

"It's the wound," she said simply.

She traced a delicate line up the centre of her body, pudenda to neck. When her hand drifted to the edge of her blouse, the fabric parted and he had a sudden realisation: her tattoo was an actual image of the wound.

"When I fuck, the wound opens and the new Mayas come out. But now it's pulling me into it. Finally."

The word 'finally' was a dying sigh.

Her pupils were entirely dilated as to make her irises seem almost black, but an edge of green seeped from around the drugged circlet of her eye. He didn't try to stop her when she went to the door.

"Why did you come here?" he said.

She smiled at him, bearing her fangs slightly, and then she left.

It wasn't until some moments later that he noticed the black leather book that she had left on the chair. It sat there like a fingerprint. Evidence of a haunting. He knew that she wouldn't be coming back. But he still felt pushed into the drift of waiting.

He later wondered what had kept him from following her.

Cowardice, he came to realise, was the primary prohibition.

He waited until he got home to open her book. He hadn't opened it at the office because besides the nagging superstitious feeling that he'd had since she'd left his office, waiting to read it was the only way he could draw out the seduction. Waiting to look at the pages was like waiting to part a lover of her last vestige of clothing. The anticipation was wonderful and terrible. He didn't realise that like any first fuck, one is always a little afraid of being disappointed.

II

The Eulogies

With this pen, I am building the cemetery to lay my lovers down. These are eulogies for all the men who fucked me into existence; for the men who fucked me out of it again. When I am done writing, I will no longer be Maya.

I will no longer be.

This is the necrology, a one-sided epistolary and the letters will be returned to the great amniotic sea with affection and fume.

The period at the end of the last sentence is the good bullet.

The shared body has driven us to war.

We are locked together bone and nerve, a perpetual fuck machine. Such is the general plight of red-lipped whores like us. But the Maya have sustained me, and I them, even as we have vied for ascendancy, for a single mind in this life. Yet we are joined at the cunt, sewn together in the body, we are forced to remain together despite all my attempts to sever the union. No cock or finger can cleave us.

We are joined at the very point where we open. Joined at the tip of the wound. The door. The Maya are the bridge, the book, the explanation and the end, and I am their mouths.

They are slowly pushing me back into my own cunt so that they can finish this business with the unyielding body. The debts have almost been paid. The journey has been marvellous and bloody and their histories are left with me here under the skin. When I finish writing, I am both unravelled and complete. When I finally go back into the wound, the tortures of this awkwardness ends. The Via Negativa is the way back in.

My lovers have been unqualified surgeons, but I chose them because rather than separate me, they connect me to her in constant rebirth. I tell myself that I hope for final severance from her, thinking that it would liberate me. But I have misunderstood freedom until now. She has been the freedom all along. The Maya have easily devoured them all. She is at first absorbed in their hatred and passion and sorrows. Ultimately though, *they* fall into the wound. Now I am left to eat the remainder of myself. Auto-communion. Spiritual masturbation. Transubstantiated cannibalism. The perfected fuck.

When Maya 30 subsumes Maya 29 she will take all the memory with her inside the wound. The narrative comes out of my pen a slow haemorrhage as I, this twenty-ninth manifestation of their projections, sees it. It is certainly a last vestige of egotism, I know, but an unavoidable sin in this dream.

The memories of the men enter my mind, flashing adjacent the cave walls like recollections of deteriorating films. In recalling them, I realise that I in turn was nothing more than a production of light and sound to them. A speeding shadow. A series of confusing edits, and then an end.

In their arms, between their teeth, willfully impaled on their bodies, the previous Maya would die and the next would come, pushing out of the orgasm, larval and wet. Waking, the new Maya would unfurl the fragile wing and flee the scene of the suicide. Self-murder followed by the confusions of love and violence. We have flown away, leaving the dead Maya behind like sacks of skin on grubby sheets, staining beds all around the world. There are bodies strewn like abandoned mattresses. Junk beds, abandoned beds waiting for the cremation. I write with gasolined ink and a match in my mouth.

At first, I thought that I was just feeling strangely disconnected from the world, but then I realised that I had actually transformed. I had become. I left my lovers someone different as affected by the exchange of scent, heat, spit and sperm. The technicians have tried to convince me that I am applying symbolism to a pathological problem, but the scientists are the ones that are pathologically dead to the subtleties of the real world. Blind. Every suicide fuck has brought me closer to the centric. Every suicide has brought me closer to fusing with her permanently so that we are immutably Maya.

It took the violence to make me aware of the metamorphosis. Pain is the way in. Pain is the way out. She is the pain. Through the lens of pain married to pleasure, I have a view of the previous Maya. The memories come to me in simultaneous symphonies of bodily recollection, yet they are fragmented and connected. They run through me like rooms in a mansion without halls. The door is my cunt.

But memory is fiction; an epic crazy quilt that I reinvent to remind myself that I am still living in this prison of Maya. The present is a fragment of a synthetic past with the obscure hope of a future. I am tired of the contrivances, weary of the hallucinogenics, anti-depressants, and fashionable forms of torture.

She is Maya 30, my soul in the amniotic drift of the future. Neomort. Neonate. She is the unborn dead — constantly coming, forever dying. She seizures inside; climactic spasms in the womb, foetal fingers dug up into the cunt, pulling out the time.

She is the first and the last, and before I go back to her inside the wound, I am going to write Maya 29 into existence.

It is necessary so that I can die.

Her handwriting worked the page in a barely controlled rage, the feeling trying to escape between the shape and slant of the letters. There was a desperation intrinsic in the slope and turn of the black ink, but he could not help but recognise a faintly hidden irony. He couldn't decide if he was being kicked or fucked. His body was making him nervous, as if it might do something unexpected. He set the book down, but left the pages open. Looking sidelong at it, he felt as if he'd left a corpse on the couch next to him with the legs spread open. The open pages of the book were like a dead cunt staring at him. When he was reading the words, the leather of the folio seemed to be like human skin, pulsating and speaking with him. Once out of his hands, the thing was dead and forbidding. He closed the journal. He considered documenting the events of the day for the sake of science, but he had long come to believe that psychiatry was a crock of shit.

He went and poured himself a drink, and then another. He stared at the amber liquid in his glass and realised that this was not stiff enough medication. He opened his phone book, looking for a vulture to come and pick him over. Early in his career he had found that the word 'doctor' attracted plenty of carrion eaters. He had a whole address book filled with their names and numbers. Almost at random, he picked a name and dialled her number. While he waited, he poured himself another shot and put the book in the bedroom, where it belonged.

Locked up.

III

Maya 1

All traces of sex and sperm were carefully doused or douched away, so we were bewildered to find it located inside our own bodies, hidden inside the sweat and stink. We knew it was *present*, but it is a different thing to actually smell the manifestation through all the disinfectant of our middle class minds. When I looked at him, I could already hear the moans of angry orgasm over the sitcom symphony of laugh tracks. His mouth was a siren and muted all the other tinny sounds of the suburban screams we were used to. He could smell me too and we had the waiting written all over us. The need to fuck was as obvious as angry welts all over our bodies and it hurt to be around each other until the operation was performed. I pushed and punched at the edges of his womb until it hurt him too much to keep me inside.

His water broke with a little shout and it spread like a rumour on the cotton percale sheets. Labour and delivery were quickly performed on the Ethan Allan twin bed, that stood like an embarrassing admission to having been his momma's boy.

We got rid of his mother, but I forget what we did with her. I think he shoved her up inside my cunt. When he fucked me, Maya 1 squeezed out of the eye of his prick, twisting and writhing her shoulders out of the opening like a cockeyed Athena setting herself free.

Our lungs filled with a half-embarrassed scream. Pity they didn't come out full bloomed and red, because then we could've avoided all the plumbing problems down the line, but the moan is a weak question. He came theatrically, shuddering like a Creem dream. Ricky. Jon. Bobby. Red white and blue boys a little short on technique. Vaseline transfusions are a good idea for the slide Home. Blood maps racing us to fourth base. America thrills. Luck be a lady tonight. Lady luck cracking the transparent film between the waking and the dead. The crack-up. Between the thighs. Another virgin squashed between the gnashing teen teeth, black juice running down his chin. Pleasure in the immediate past. Consanguinity. Cousin to the return. Purple bitten lip. I saw the sadness coming in like a red storm low over the little bed.

He didn't notice the transmigration of souls.

None of them do. My body has become an inconsequential but necessary tool in desperate expeditions, a compass pointing them inward towards the tropical mystery.

Maya 1, newborn, stood at the foot of the bed and licked herself clean, watching us fumble around the fuck as if the act itself was an obstacle rather than the object. I was here, though I was the old body too. I lifted its hips up off the sheets and every time he lifted up a little and then came down harder, I felt the wound open and the umbilicus snake its way between me and her. Connected through the cunt. My former persona was afterbirth. Maya was just a cunt squeezing and breathing and watching the marvellous creature, Maya 1 indulge and acquire the experience. The Maya are the receptacles for the memory. I am just a cunt.

6 am. . . debris of the ego was strewn around the bed. Wanted to go home. Should've been there hours ago. I got up and left the old skin behind on the bed with him. I left the dead twin hanging on a hook. Bones poked through the tender new flesh like the ribs of a shipwrecked boat. Like the ribs of a jackal. The constant reminder of the goddamn rib. Adam. First apple.

Capture the moment, Kodak Thief, I said.

This is our moment in the landscape of adolescence. Splitting atoms, hymens. Splitting hairs.

Virgin. It's a relative term.

He lifted himself up over the body, shoulders hunched — a half-assed Dracula demanding — where's the blood? He reached down and brought up clean fingers. Where's the blood?

He was my first suicide.

Where's the blood? he insisted.

I couldn't explain the appalling lack of proof. I lay there titless, skinless, bloodless. The protection of Maya 1 was already seeping out of the bedroom. Most of the Maya had very short lives. The half-life of an orgasm, the half-life of a soul transmigrating, born out of cocks' heads, dying into the wound that is the umbilicus.

I remember the creation of the wound. A hole bigger than a shapeless foldless cunt. Useless when not fucking, except for filling up with letters and photographs and a few books. His finger searched again, but tired of the complicated navigations. Cheaping out, he took his cock like a curved forceps and yanked the last bit out of me, bringing Maya 1 with it all.

I am sitting in this hotel so that I can write the cemetery of dead lovers. This is a eulogy to all the men I fucked because they have fucked me into and out of existence.

You never forget your first apple, Maya 1 said and then she died leaving me there with him. Her dying words.

Silence is the only rescue. Suicide is cheap.

That was the night I was turned out. Maya 1. Maya Magdalena, Patron Saint of the Suburban Sluts.

I went to school the next morning and said you can shove *Catcher in the Rye* and *Hamlet* up my cunt because they don't mean shit to me.

Most of the times their bodies turned into inconsequential borders that simply had to be crossed. It was the blue spark of cock to cunt, that caused the birthing of these other Maya. After the new Maya had been born and died, my lovers seemed useless — problematic even.

The wound opened like a yawn when I came and I needed their fingers and lips and teeth to pry it open wider still. Now, nearing the end of the cycle I only need one more lover to birth the last Maya, Maya 30. With her, I can finish off this suicide life, these lives parcelled into rooms of distorted memory inside the skin mansion. The body tires, the tits weary. The house sags. There are only so many times a door will open, the skin parting to the universe and its crushing entropy. I am looking for the gravity-free kiss. I am looking for the union and the end. Every morning I wake, and the earth's air, Planet Disease, pumps up the remaining shell of my decaying armature with oxygen and advertising. I am sick of vulgar Planet Disease and its compulsion towards entertainment. Breasts fill out, and the belly fleshes. After every suicide, I bathe away the residual effects of the former Maya, Maya 1, Maya 2, Maya 3 and so on, running down the drains like a vague filth of my former self. These are the eulogies to those Maya.

I am Maya 29, waiting to become. The 30th. The last.

IV

Malpractice

the doorman rang, and Lazar experienced a piercing but familiar moment of despair. It plummeted down the centre of his body and he killed its career by throwing back the rest of his drink. He poured another and watched the door.

His profession left him sceptical about finding any kind of solace or happiness in intimacy or anywhere else. Using his science, he had objectively deduced that most people's search for union with another produced pain. It was usually so excruciating and repeated that one had to wonder why the wounded bodies didn't just expire out of sadness. But mostly they endured, and with his advice, they careened forward towards more and more failed experiments. When he was younger and more ambitious, he had made attempts at proving wrong the voice inside. The invective that claimed: *life is suffering*. And though Dr Lazar was meant to help his patients, it was never written into any contract that he was himself supposed to be complete, or even trying to become so. Surely most of his patients happily deluded themselves regarding any question about his mental health. To them it was a fundamental truth that he was unequivocally sane. He had never made that promise to anyone, but he didn't perceive his condition as an illness; his personal pain had become colourless and undistinguished to him.

The white noise of his patients' problems, both the epic and the minutiae, had murdered his sensitivity. All the Ophelias, and Jesus's, all the neurotic divas and nightmare-hunted Oedipal casualties that had limped through his consultation room during years of psychiatric practice had left him dead to most of their seductive tricks. It was all the shame that had finally killed his compassion. Certainly he had heard some baroque fantasies, and of course every kind of confession imaginable. He found himself hoping to hear them come to a screeching halt at the frontier of their own morality and then fly over it. But it never happened. The shame prevented it. Upon reflection that was what Maya had lacked. Shame.

Maya resonated in his memory as the first woman he had met in a long time who had clearly not looked to him to help her, save her or fuck her. Her brief presence signalled a kind of devolution to him. She had thrown him back towards the remembrance of authentic desires. And then reading the first pages of her book had reminded him of a time when sex had been something other than a sedative.

The woman rapped lightly on the door and he heaved himself from the couch. When he opened it, she smiled at him with hesitation. When he saw her standing there vulnerable and anxious, he felt a feather of subtle contempt brush against his entire body. A wave of something not meriting the passionate energy of rancour, but he briefly observed that in the last few years he was more often than not affected with this sense of ersatz hatred.

He found himself wondering for the hundredth time, what kind of woman would arrive at his house so late in the evening without the perks of preliminary theatrics? No dinner, no charming conversation. No foreplay. She probably deserved something, but his drive to fuck away the pain was more intense than any concern for her. She too needed him for other reasons, reasons too complicated and banal for him to worry himself with in any authentic way. She said hello and stepped past him, walking into his apartment like a *mea culpa*.

He waited in the hall, his back to her, listening to her making a drink. He closed the door and asked her how she had been, and she shrugged her coat off in answer. He wanted to tell her that he was glad she came, but he wasn't. He wanted to tell her he was grateful for the service that she was going to perform, but that was too naked. He was ashamed and then felt slightly embarrassed for his feelings of soft disgust. Whatever weak attraction he felt for her was fed by this feeling and he wondered how transcendence in these matters had eluded him. He knew the formulae. He was aware of the pathos intrinsic to the psychological operettas of peccadilloes.

Where's your husband? he asked instead.

She smiled, but didn't answer.

I came, didn't I? she said after a while.

He smiled. Not yet, he said.

Let's not talk about him. She moved towards him.

He nodded, and stepped away from her approach. He fixed himself another drink. He asked her if she was hungry and she said yes.

For you.

He winced inwardly at the clichéd language that seemed to accompany all his sexual encounters.

You, he said, for lack of anything else.

Yes, she said and came towards him.

He didn't move, waiting for her to come.

She wrapped her hands around his waist from behind and pushed her pelvis forward. He felt the angular saw of her bones. He wished he could meet a woman with a real ass. The women that frequented his life were vainly caught in some transitory web of dieting, surgery. Psychotherapy. He fought off feeling the panic her body inspired in him. It was an unpleasant chaos that made him want to push her hard. He turned. When they kissed, he listened for the quiet snap inside. This event was something that started to happen after his divorce. He located its nexus during his first affair with a patient. There was a distinct separation that occurred upon contact and nothing he could do would prevent this disassociative rent from happening. It had ceased to bother him, and now he simply observed the quiet series of dilations and emptiness opening below his feet. Touching forced the alienations — of body from self, sensation from feeling — events that had become the preliminary machinations to his sexual life. He was constantly disappointed that his lovers didn't notice, or that they could not be bothered with the implications of such a problem. His affairs had turned mercenary in the past few years. It was something that just seemed to happen when he let go his tentative grip on the hope of a contented union with women. A contented union with any other human.

She pushed her fingers into his neck and said, you're tight.

He could smell her acrylic false fingernails.

Let me give you a —

No, he said and grabbed her hand abruptly. Suddenly, he didn't want to give into the weary habits of this affair. She was startled but didn't say anything.

No. He said again and turned around and pushed his mouth against her neck. She giggled a little and the sound enraged him, as if she was mocking his feeble attempt at sincerity. The laugh told him to forget it, but the drive to connect with a body persisted and he pulled her harder to him. He pulled her head around so that he could watch the tensile stretch of tendon against neck. He thought of Maya's neck. He pushed into her mouth with his, as if he meant to find something under her tongue. He tugged and pulled at her clothes and she tried to pull away to help him but he grabbed her arms hard behind her back with one hand while he lifted her tasteful dress with the other. She seemed a little surprised, but not afraid. He was her psychiatrist. He wasn't going to hurt her.

He didn't necessarily want to hurt her, he just wanted to injure her into feeling something. He wanted to use her body as a conduit to something else. He wanted to use her cunt and tits as facilitators to help him get back to some little piece of meaning. He was filled with a persistent nagging to return to a time when all it took for him to feel electrically charged and connected to a woman was an inadvertent whisper of knees touching, to a place where kissing a lover was as powerful as an orgasm, and all sensations were equally magnificent.

Maya had gone off like an alarm in his office. Her strange presence had alerted his body to some reminder, some hidden clue in the muscle memory. The reminder of a push and will towards something that he was yet unsure of. He deluded himself into believing that the answer was possibly hidden inside the body of the woman in front of him, and the fact that it was clearly such a self-deception made him angry.

She said something that he didn't hear. He wasn't listening to her words, just her body. He put his ear to her back, his head resting between the razor sharps of her scapula that jutted like brittle rich-bird wings under the film of her dress. He felt an unfamiliar bile when he heard nothing. Even when he spat on his palm, lubed his cock and shoved it into her asshole, he still heard nothing but a buzzing silence come up from this empty vessel. She screamed, letting the sound out like a controlled bleeding.

You're hurting me, she gasped.

He kept his head against her back and gripped her jutting hips. He watched himself disappear into her.

No, really you're hurting me, she breathed.

Good, he said.

Yeah, she said. It's good, baby.

Shut up, he said quietly. Just shut your mouth and let me fuck you. Just let me shut you up.

Yes, she said. Yes doctor. Yes — she started to say his name and he reached around and put his palm over her mouth. The other hand kept time moving more deeply into the tight hole which suggested a possibility of formlessness, but her body was not delivering what he desired, because her body was getting in the way. She was the wrong body. They all were. His hips moved pneumatically in and out of her. He didn't want to hear his name come out of her mouth. Ever.

The orgasm left him feeling anaemic. Without speaking, he ordered her to leave so he could tend the insults to his body. She looked wounded and he was glad. He'd never fucked her in the ass before, and he had no intention of doing it again. He hadn't liked the closeness of her skin around his. He hadn't liked the pulsing of that muscle around his. The sound of the door shutting behind her was a little death in the apartment. When he heard the elevator doors close, he felt some relief.

He sat and wondered exactly when had he lost the sense of sexual vigilance that informed so much of his earlier life? He couldn't help but see it as pathetic relenting. But Maya and her strange little book of scribbled eulogies had started a weed growing in his belly and he could feel its strange but not entirely unfamiliar seeding. He sat on the couch and thought about opening the book again, and the thought was ambiguously obscene. As though he were considering lifting a little girl's skirt. He didn't like the association or the muted erotic feelings he had that went along with that picture. He went into to the bedroom, and thought to unlock the drawer where he kept the SIG. The dull black Teflon body of the gun pleased him. And now the worn leather book lay next to it and it seemed right. Looking at the blank cover of the book reminded him of her blank eyes, and he felt an obscure twinge of sadness bruise his consciousness. He closed the drawer and locked it. Lazar fell into an uneasy sleep thinking before he drifted, that tomorrow he would. Tomorrow he would look into her.

V

She Lies Waiting

*H*e was bothered by the dream for the length of the afternoon and he found that the agitation was a welcome relief to the usual tedium of his work. Most people mistakenly believed that psychiatry would be endlessly fascinating, and there was a time when he thought that as well. But that was a long time ago.

He had been troubled after the woman left his apartment the night before, but it didn't really affect him until he undressed completely and went to take a shower. He noticed a little bit of dried blood on his flaccid penis and he simply held it in his hand and stared at it. It reminded him of a dead flower. She had left this piece of herself behind despite all his efforts to leave no trace of her ever having come. Similarly she had been sent home with his imprint painfully pressed on the inside of her body. He examined his feelings as he looked at his penis. He felt nothing in particular about it except annoyance at his carelessness about the details. What did disturb him was his increasing lack of affect. He washed and went to bed.

Maya was not in his dream, at least not appearing the way she had looked in his office that previous afternoon. He wrote down what he remembered of the dream. He noted that he had found himself in a small room which was most certainly medical, but at first he didn't notice any sign of it being a consultation room. It seemed much more forbidding than the most terrific surgical theatres, but there were no tools around that would identify it as such. Yet he remembered that it had the familiar smell of bodily fluids masked by isopropyl alcohol.

She said his first and last name and his body reacted before he could think. He felt an excitement that was odd, but one he recognised. He felt virginal and electric. When he turned, he felt it was her but it did not appear to be her.

There were two women sitting side by side on a metal examination table. They were completely hairless and the lack of hair on their heads made their faces beautiful and perversely impish. At first their faces frightened him a little because he could not immediately recognise what was askew until he realised that they had no eyebrows. The absence of pubic hair made their cunts seem childish and strange in contrast to their womanly breasts and hips. They were joined together in some way that was obscured at first. He approached and saw the external stretch of flesh that joined them. He felt that there was a specific procedure that he was meant to perform, but he felt uncertain as to which one it was. He thought that perhaps he was meant to separate them and he was concerned.

I am not a surgeon, he said.

Yes, you are, they replied

What have they done to your hair? he asked.

They were looking for the mark. The devil's mark. They've found twenty-nine. They shared a voice, but both their lips moved.

I've come to hear your confession.

I have nothing to confess, they said calmly.

Maya? he said, feeling suddenly desperate to get closer to her. To identify her, but he felt that he was at cross-purposes. He had been sent to get something from them, or do something to them and his well-being seemed to depend on the procedure. But he couldn't remember who sent him or what he was supposed to get.

I have come to hear your confession, he repeated dumbly.

You want inside, the girls said.

Yes, he said. Yes, his body said. His cock filled with blood and a flush ringed his neck. He suddenly realised he was inside the feeling that he thought he'd forgotten; that sensation of newness and fear, the remembrance of life connected to sex. It was so much more vast than the neutral appetite that he had grown used to, an appetite which had to be fed mechanically. He was wearing a uniform of some sort that he couldn't remember upon waking.

Come. Come in, they said. It was not a welcoming, but the statement of inevitability, and so he went to them.

They held out their arms to him, their expression mutually dead. Their eyes simply reflected the atrocity of their deformity.

You're joined. He heard his own voice far away. He came closer to them, and fingered the stretch of flesh that connected them just below the floating rib. Touching the anomaly aroused him.

Yes. We're all joined. You. Me. Them. Joined. Yes we are.

Their skin felt slightly damp to the touch, not sweating but as if steam was rising from within their flesh.

As he lightly stroked the connection of flesh between them, he felt a sudden terrifying pull from their centre. He studied them as they started to spasm slightly. It was vaguely grotesque, and he wanted to wake, but he was captivated by their fierce magnetic pull.

At first he thought that his hands were being pulled inside their vaginal openings, the soft flesh cleaving and closing around his wrist. The warm tissue closed around his fingers and the warm wet surrounded his hand as he felt it rise against his chest and abdomen. When he was able to, he opened his eyes and found that he was being heaved into two large cavities, each opening at the centre of the twins. It appeared to be an incision that had a vacuuming power. The smell of sex choked the small examination room, and he started to loose the sense of his bodily parameters. The sensation was terrifying but not entirely unpleasant. He was caught between resisting and simply allowing it to happen. The only barrier that kept him from going all the way inside the hole was the fact that he was meant to complete some task that seemed imperative. He pulled his body away.

They didn't even seem to notice that he had left their bodies. They were joined at the mouth in a kiss that filled him with jealous longing. Between their lips they passed a black pearl. Their bodies were still open and he could clearly see into their bodily cavities. Blood seeped out around their legs and dripped off the stainless steel examination table. When they saw him looking at them, they both reached around and virtuously pulled their skin back around to the middle, averting their eyes and hiding the wound. Their skins fused and sealed shut.

You want everybody's secrets, they hissed. It sounded almost like an accusation.

No, he said. I want the — he didn't know what he wanted, but theirs was an emptiness that had left him needing. He didn't want to hear confessions, he needed something but the words and specific desires eluded him. Other men entered the small room. They wore medical masks and they surrounded the twins. Terrible things were going to happen, and he felt somehow responsible for it.

A man in a mask stood next to him and said, It would have happened even if you heard their confessions. Your methods are useless.

He woke feeling soiled and frustrated. Betrayed and disappointed. Throughout the day he tried to recall other times that he had experienced this feeling , because it wasn't entirely unfamiliar. It finally occurred to him that he felt very similarly after the first night he'd had sex when he was a teenager. When he lost his virginity he did feel as if he had actually mislaid something, and the recaptured memory saddened him in a surprising burst of sentimentality that annoyed and fascinated him. He was surprised by the enduring nature of such emotions.

Even though he knew on a rational level that she would not be coming back to his office, he could not resist giving into momentary flashes of hope that she might return to retrieve the book and free him from the compulsion to read it.

He felt a tremendous relief when the last patient had been ushered to the door with a prescription slip clutched in her hand. Rather than type up his notes in the office directly following the day's sessions, he instead found himself anxious to get home. She was waiting for him in the drawer, lying calmly next to the .357.

VI

Heroina

I needed a more entertaining murderer than my last. It was one of the demands that the new body was making.

The obscenity of sentimentality repulsed the new Maya, and because of this the pimply boys fell dead around her; stiff with rigormortis under the heel of my black boots. The new body had been ushered in without sympathy or holes. Except of course for the wound.

The boys circled us; confused vultures that were rendered helpless without the carrion of corsages, proms and sappy wines — those sweet ready-made seductions boys just outside the urban sprawl fed on in those days. I don't know what they need now.

I told them they were going to have to draw blood to get anywhere with me and when they heard that they tended to faint. It became clear that it was going to be difficult to find an unusually gifted sadist among the adolescents of my tribe; or at least ones that had some mindful creativity about their cruelty.

I waited alone in my room sharpening my tongue and pumping gin into my veins. Maya 2 was a black-boozed flower writing hideous odes to pains imagined and real. Without a mouth there was no other recourse but to write it down. The piss and shit and cum and blood dribbled out from under my fingernails. I gave off the stink of some unidentifiable bile; a spleen perfume that would draw a certain kind of dog to sniff my ass.

I wandered across stretches of skin in a drunken boat. Mapless, I navigated with numbed hands and my wound. New humiliating hungers jutted out of my body under the tightness of sweaters and inside the seams of darkling jeans. Maya 2 carried the quiet burden of secrets and I adapted to my new twin's body until I was her and she me joined below the rib. Joined at the bottle. Joined at the cunt — the source of all wounds.

Where's the blood? he had said, and the 2nd Maya was born.

The language of my new manifestation was composed of partial sentences, and I drifted from word to word as though I was constantly on the verge of falling asleep. I was caught in the midway point between waking and dying, and I held onto the raw edge of the new body. The odour I gave off was unpleasant enough to be sent to the professionals. They tried to clean me up so I wouldn't smell so deviant. The technicians used their conspicuous and crooked methods to try and modify Maya 2 into something better smelling. Something more pleasing to the ear. Something a little more refined to look at, but the wound was a screamer and a bleeder and it would not be silenced or tourniqued. It will not be until the end.

They wanted to reinstate Maya 1 because she was easier to fuck with.

"That Maya suicided." I told them. "She is lying dead at the scene of the crime. The body is hidden under a child's twin bed."

Music was strangling the air in LA — music more toxic than the smog and the booze. The sounds of modish anarchy started to poke tiny needle holes into the body. Letting the sound in. Letting night in.

X. FEAR. SUICIDAL TENDENCIES.

The body contact of hostile hormonal dementia in night-clubs relieved some of the tension of the enforced chastity, but the need to fuck was growing like rumour spreading in the body. The anatomically incorrect desires sprawled like a sweating rain forest. Already the impact of the first suicide was muting and fading. He had been absorbed into the wound and the need for a second was starting to turn hot and viral-like mutating disgraces I kept hidden in the pockets of my coats. The tangled scream of the music, the watery odourless vodka, cheap leather and sweat were causing grand mal pseudo-seizures, and I cruised and frothed all over LA in an elliptical slam. I was searching for my next murderer. My next lover.

I found him by following the trail of white, the powder and needle path to the next crime scene. He stood there with dark glasses and an accent waiting to make the new Maya.

When he had come home from work, he had avoided going directly to the book. He read his mail. A letter from his ex-wife lay unopened on the table, as interesting to him as the bills and junk mail. He prowled around his house, annoyed by all the nice things. He felt cagey and anxious, but he was enjoying the low level hum of anticipation. He opened a bottle of wine. Listened to his messages.

"Simon, I just wanted to call to say…" The woman's voice

who had come to him last night filled his apartment. He snapped off the machine and erased her.

"Simon, this is Anna…" Lazar smiled and he felt his body relax noticeably. Her voice was like a little flower of normalcy, a daisy in a field of carnivorous flowers. "Jade and I are having a dinner party on Saturday. William St. John is coming to dinner. He's expressed some interest in representing Jade. We're very excited and your presence is required. Bring some wine. 8:00. No is not an option. See you then."

He immediately wrote *Dinner — Anna* in his date book. He felt a sense of relief in hearing her voice. Anna was one of his oldest friends; a woman who loved him deeply, but who had never wanted anything from him except sincere friendship.

William St. John. He remembered that Catherine, his ex-wife, had mentioned William St. John on a number of occasions when she had been working as an editor. Based on what she said, St. John was easily one of the most powerful young literary agents in the business. He recalled that Catherine had said more about him, but it was at a point in their relationship where he had ceased listening to her. He didn't like the association that the name St. John had with Catherine, but he shrugged it off.

He felt that there was some cowardice in his sudden relief at hearing Anna's familiar voice – comfort his body immediately drove towards. Despite his intellectual desire to get back to the book, there was a nagging urge to leave it locked away. When he considered opening the book, a disturbing feeling of fragmentation, of uncertain ruin flapped around his head in whispers and far away groans. He pushed the superstitions away with annoyance.

He drank another glass of wine, took a shower and finally went to the locked dresser and opened it. The book seemed different than he had remembered. Smaller.

He opened the first page again and noticed for the first time a frontispiece that said:

The Book of Wounds

He could have sworn it wasn't there when he first had opened the book. There was a childish and obscene drawing that accompanied the frontispiece: an ink line drawing of a woman with an enormous cunt that ran the entire length of her torso. He felt a certain twinge settle in his sacrum as the nervous twitch rushed down his spine. The girl in the picture was entirely bald. Including a lack of eyebrows.

He closed the book again, and then reopened it, wondering how he could have missed it the first time he had cracked it open. He told himself that either the pages stuck or he had simply flipped past it very quickly. That would explain the imprinting of the image on his unconscious memory. That would explain the hairless Siamese twins in his dream. He felt slightly relieved at that quick machination of his profession, even if he didn't believe it in any authentic way.

He smelled the book. It had the damp smell of worn leather. He sniffed it again, and then felt embarrassed at the vulgar undertones of his action. He never really empathised with the compulsion to smell a woman's underwear. He didn't feel shame, but more anger at himself for being so ridiculously taken with another in the parade of neurotics that had stumbled through his office.

He carried the book with him and sat down on the edge of the bed, recalling that her visit had seemed so calm, so pre-arranged. She had entered his reality with a poise that left him uneasy. He was surprised by the realisation that during all his years of practising psychiatry he had actually enjoyed observing the trepidation and fear that most of his patients entered his consultation room bearing like gifts to bestow. Often hopeful that their torment was the most elaborate and pain-filled. That their problems were far more intense than any of the other patients he treated. Lazar had grown used to watching the whole drama with an amused distance. But he was mildly surprised that it had taken Maya's visit to make that ugly fact apparent to him. He shrugged it away, but it didn't matter because she wouldn't be coming back and the feeling would fade. He would simply skim the book, put it in a file and forget about it.

Opiated is the juice in married men and sweet was his promise of the numb. He had a wife, but he wasn't married to her; he was married to it. He shone like a knife on the bleached streets of Los Angeles and I picked him up without hesitation. The body of Maya 2 was wasting away, and the mistral winds from my cunt were ruining thigh and skirt. The itch to die was bothering the body into non-existence.

I knew he was the one the minute the smoke came out of his nose and rather than get down to the crime immediately, we minced around each other; dark-eyed jackals weaving in and out between packs of mongrel addicts sniffing each other out like host and cell. The seduction rite was drugged and distracted. Fragments of queer flirtations confused the body, uncertain if they were threats or promises. After I found him, I trailed him for weeks, following the constant jangle of ringing phones, and the jagged parade of jonesing freaks. He romanced me without removing his black glasses or gloves, a perfect criminal for a low-budget crime.

I liked watching his plump wife understand the addiction. I liked watching the amorality slide around on the dinner table, her husband's cloven Italian leather toes shoved in my tight crotch. Certainly the traits of Maya 3 had started to show themselves even before the actual suicide of Maya 2. Maya 3 was overdue. He unbuttoned the safety pins holding my lips together. His wife turned back to watch the slow-motion jerk of the crash, slack-jawed and drunk. She seemed dowdy and sloppy under my black-crafted spell. I wanted to tell her that I was only using her husband to commit suicide. She could have him back after I was done. But her edges were absorbed amongst the other wolves that roamed the scene. She vanished under their claws and coke.

We mouthed meaningless sounds towards each other under the quadraphonic metal riffs. He finally bit me as we stood around the swirling shit storm in the doorway of the Whiskey A Go-Go, black-hooded vampires brushing against our foreplay. He put his teeth in my neck and dragged me into his car. The black rubber wings unfurled and he drove his chariot fast towards his shooting gallery hidden in the ersatz green somewhere on the edge of the hot sprawl.

Bodies were strewn around the floor of the house like filthy laundry. Their needles and pipes glinted like stars in the candlelight. He daintily picked his way over the land of nod, his fingers locked around my wrist like a handcuff. He could see in the dark with his black glasses on. Cool, I said, stepping over the human detritus and spoons.

Already heavily medicated, he offered anasthaesias that would clear away the effects of cheap booze and smokes. I'm going to blow out your speakers baby girl, he said. White light, he said. What he was offering was more than punk noir or crime. He was offering to punch a new hole into my black with his body, with his fist and needle. He promised to off me. Cool, I said, edging up closer to the other side.

I slipped around him easily, bouncing off his pelvis and lip like a chromed ball in a pachinko machine. He waited like a pin in the game, letting my body ricochet off his. She stood motionless, simply holding the crystal rock in one hand, foil and his cock in the other. Kissing him, feeling his cock through the armour of our jeans made the drive to kill Maya 2. I was caught in a blinding snow storm that I drove my tits and ass through, tilting towards the fuck with all my weight. The edges of her body were giving way to the sharper, meaner metal of Maya 3's shape and form. The filigree of her fuck was razor-edged and high. With a morphia arc and needle he pulled her out. I left Maya 2 behind on the floor like a shoe blown away from the foot after a shot-gun blast.

Put your ring on my lips, I said, in front of his wife and she turned her head.

He put his gold wedding band in my mouth. I smiled and I swallowed it. He slapped my face, and when I felt the warmth of blood on the corner of my lip, I knew. The wound woke. The steel edges of Maya 3 kicked and poked at the decaying flesh of the former self.

I'm going to have to go in there and get that out of you now, he said, unbuckling his belt.

I waited fingering his crystal.

Come here.

I came forward, the body in front of me like a bouquet of drooping flowers, wilted petals of flesh hanging over my hands like a bunch of question marks. He snatched my arm tapping the soft surface, searching for the hole but couldn't find one that we could both recognise as an entry. He was going to have to make a new one.

Tie me off, I said. Tourniquet the wound before I die.

Shut up, he said, and turn around. I want to give it to you before I give it to you.

Yeah, I said. Cool.

He rubbed some cocaine on the tip of his cock and said, suck it. I placed my numbed tongue on the shaft. More spit, he said. The phone rang.

Shit, he snarled, and grabbed my hair. I was on the floor in front of him and he held my head like he was readying to baptise me, or as if he'd just finished the rite. I still had the tip of his cock in my mouth, the back of my throat and lips felt stupid with the coke. I did not want to smile because it seemed so serious, but he looked clownish with his pink cock hanging out of his zipper. The grin edged around the coke-numbed flesh and he yanked my hair harder. His cock was going limp. The phone stopped ringing, but the applause on the television resumed even louder.

What's funny?

This, I said.

He held me by my collar, yanking the choke-chain fiercely. The pop of sudden strangulation surprised me and when the oxygen rushed back into my throat the thrill was titanic.

Do it again, I said, offering my neck up pathetically.

He laughed. A budding pervert, he said.

The phone started ringing again and he walked out of the room leaving me there with the laugh tracks and the cadavers. And this decaying body of Maya 2 tenaciously holding onto her last minutes.

Don't go, I said.

Shut up, he said, not looking over his shoulder.

I waited, kneeling in front of the flea-bitten couch counting the diamonds of my fishnets. I waited staring at the rock of coke glowing like Southern California Kryptonite. I waited, the need to get rid of Maya 2 making me sick. He came back minutes later and stood in the doorway watching me. I guess he was devising the best way to do it. Finally he started to come in for the kill, kissing me hard.

Come here, bella. Come here.

He seemed relaxed and I was disappointed. I wanted him to

fuck me when he still had the fear. Now I was going to have to antagonise him. Whenever he answered the phone a calm came over him, making him almost human for a few minutes. A promise of a sale was like a small hit of valium and he could relax his body against the marathon of anxiety for a moment. It was as if he had already climaxed and he was letting himself doze inside some meaningless fuck before the fear came on again. He was a lousy addict, not ever really figuring out the cycles of fear and arousal, and the terror usually edged inside before he could get some sort of numbing agent in between him and it. We were alike, enjoying that little sensation of terror, using it just to remind ourselves how good it felt to get out from under it for the duration of an orgasm or a shot.

This is boring. I'm leaving, I said, getting up off my knees.

Boredom was the cardinal sin. Boredom was a condemnation that would incite him to an act of retribution.

He grabbed my collar and said, you're not going anywhere, bitch.

I felt the wound tingle and stretch. Wet dripped out from between the nylon holes of my fishnets.

Yeah, man. This sucks, I said.

He pulled me up to my feet hard until I was standing on the steel-toed tips. Industrial toe shoes for a ballerina slut in black. He let go and I fell back a little. He sat down on the couch and lit a cigarette. I stood there awkwardly in front of him, the fear coming on.

Take off your clothes, he said. I unbuttoned my jeans in one motion.

Slower! he barked.

One of the cadavers moved on the floor. Hey don't shout man, it said.

Shut the fuck up, he yelled back and then trained his black glasses on me.

What the fuck are you waiting for? Get your fucking clothes off.

The cords in my neck tightened. Maya 2 was straining for some last gasp of ascendancy. Her dying words were like second thoughts. But I had already swallowed his ring, and there it was like a tacit agreement between us. He had the right to go in and fish it out. I stepped out of my jeans and left them behind like a little pool of spittle on the wood floor. He reached out and pulled the fishnets with an easy swipe and pulled the old flesh with it.

I stood in front of him naked, a stretch of waxy wound waiting to remould around his body. I would cast myself on his cock. He lit another cigarette and watched me standing shifting foot to foot vaguely humiliated. He exhaled loudly and said, Now, Come here. When I came closer, he leaned past my shoulder and put out his cigarette. His hair brushed against my cheek and I whispered in his ear.

Kill it.

And he did.

He pulled me on top of him and arranged my legs around his hips because I didn't know how to do it myself. He seemed to like the fact that I let him push me puppet-like around the shape and form of his desires however they occurred to him moment to moment. I don't remember the nipples or the inside of my thigh, parts of the body unrecognisable to those Maya. The early Maya were just the holes, or the absence of them. I was my need for holes. I had to let the light in and Maya 2 out.

He reached down between my legs and tickled the edges of my cunt for a moment, but did not dally there. Quickly he moved his finger past the tiny smooth expanse of the perineum. Beyond that anatomical point, I wasn't sure what existed. I was only cunt and mouth. My asshole was an embarrassment that was only partially acknowledged when taking a shit. His fingers weren't pleasuring me; they were just a series of hot confusions tangling up my sensory expectations. He put my hands on his shirt, my fingers around the buttons, all skill reduced to babyish motions. I simply mimicked his fingers and his face. I reminded myself that I needed this, I needed to use his body and I would go through any machination to get there. I had yet to understand the pleasure aspect of the bargain.

Perhaps I was wiser then because fucking was reduced to a series of power exchanges that were meted and exacted in mercenary bargains.

The more aroused he got, the more power he infused my body with. There was always the moment in which I might close up around him. That he might go in and not come out alive. Always a possibility.

He helped me undo each button on his shirt, his eyes drooping slightly more with every inch that my hand got closer to his cock. He put his hands over mine and aided me in the task of getting him out of his pants. When his cock was freed, he put his fingers around the stiff base and then grabbed my hand too. He raised it to his mouth and spat on it. I observed each action through the crooked lens of my dying body, giving up pieces of Maya 2 with every strange new gesture that he performed.

He lifted me easily around his hips and I clung to his neck, my body already broken down into useless parts that he would have to manipulate to get what he needed out of it. His hand rested lightly on the small of my back and he held me in place, poised over the tip of his cock. He reached into his pocket with his other hand and retrieved a small amber bottle.

Quickly, bella. Inhale.

My asshole bloomed in a powerful burst, the petals of sphincter and muscle unfurling in a sudden rush. An amyl nitrate rose, I opened at the centre, the fire of stem and thorn shooting up through my middle. He pushed me hard over his prick and with a final sigh of Maya 2 slipped out my asshole along with the blood and shit.

The tip of his cock came up through my throat, pushing her death throw out, and he caught it in his mouth. The wound spread and opened, and Maya 3 pushed forth, metal-limbed and alert. The dilations of her new holes seized and opened against his body. He growled and bit the fleshy part of the back of her neck. He tore into the flesh, his body shaking in a false rage. Without stopping the velocity of his hip motion, he looked down between them, and saw a discrete stripe of blood bead against the little scar of shadow between them. He laughed like a proud papa.

There's blood here.

She noticed the wonder in his voice, as if he were saying *I do. I am.*

Yes, she said. Yes. Fuck me. The windows of the house blew out and shattered glass rained down on them. The candles flickered and were snuffed in the *S* of her yes.

He grabbed the freshly fleshed out hips, suddenly as if he needed her, hanging on the child's body like she was the Rock of Ages. Maya 3 laughed at him and let him. As if he suddenly sensed the shift in the power game, he tried to grab her hair again, but she bit his hand and he nearly threw her body off him. A frustrated frenzy drove his body and she pressed her thighs into his, watching the viscera from the wound drip and dribble on his belly. He slowed his thrust and without letting go of her, he leaned forward and grabbed a syringe that had been lying in wait on the table.

Now, bella.

Yeah, man. Cool, she said.

Still inside her asshole, he tied her off. The needle prick was a tiny scream inside a bigger whisper and then almost immediately her body pitched into the red velvet drift. The needle dangled at the bend of her arm, the flesh there virgin and pure, and her back arched to allow him deeper sway into her. He pushed her body up and down over his until he was too tired to watch the beauty of her nod. He came inside her nausea, shouting fuck when he orgasmed; the word an empty wolf wail, white-hued and glassy. He yanked her failing body off his cock just as the arc of semen jettisoned from the eye. It fell in a long stream against the cheek of her ass and then rained down against his stomach, mixing there with the blood from her asshole. The wound cleaved and parted and Maya 3 came.

He had deflowered her veins, and this was enough for both of them. There was blood between their bodies: evidence of the second suicide.

When we pushed out of the wound, I licked myself clean, plucked his wedding ring out of my asshole and got up to find a new home. I was. I had become again, Maya 3 bloodsoaked and ass weary. Before I left I meant to take the works and some H. Without moving, he said, leave that. I leaned over him and took his dark glasses off his face and was not surprised to find that he had no eyes.

Her writing was stifling him, as if her words were sucking the oxygen out of his body in a slow excruciating draw. He felt speedy, a little dirty, and unnerved by the subtle changes of the book since he had last read it. It felt physically different, the tones slightly changed but they were still of her. He flipped back to the first page, trying to avoid the gruesome epitaph, but there it was like a challenge.

He found that he was anxiously aroused by what he had just read; an odd excitement both physical and clinical. The shift in tenses that Maya used, if they were not poetic conceits, indicated a serious pathological disturbance. Yet that interest was dwarfed by the formless jealousy he felt against the man who had plunged into her, rudely plucking the blood and tissue from her body. He paused, wondering if she had offered him her ass, what would he have done and realised that he would have done much the same. He would have pushed into her, and held her mouth shut and fucked her until she was limp, hanging like a rag doll on the end of his prick. However, the thought was unsatisfying and ridiculous.

He wanted her to come to him again, and started to devise methods for trying to find her. He told himself it wouldn't be impossible, that she had mentioned seeing another doctor, that she... he stopped himself. His desire was motivating him towards a manic surge. It had been so long since he had listened to the true music of insanity, he had forgotten its contagious riff.

His days were generally filled with the banalities of crippling loneliness, self-hatred, guilt, and the shame, the persevering poisonous shame. But her words were having a consumptive effect on him and he knew that even he could be pulled into their sway. It would not be difficult to believe in the private cosmology of the girl. He wouldn't find her, he told himself. He didn't need to. She was already in his grip.

Most of the confessions that he heard lacked a certain kind of coherence. He found that his patients were generally unaware of the epics they were writing with their experiences and tales. Nor were they usually aware of the networking of filigree within their own interpretations of the tales. It usually took a good doctor to lend structure to their narratives, but he wasn't a good doctor any more.

Maya's book had a quality that suggested she was aware of the fabric she was weaving. It was something to hang her mania on, and he found her peculiar arrangement very attractive. This desire made him feel sick, and he threw the book aside as if he was pushing a desperate lover out of his life.

He stood and went into the other room and when he got there he suddenly didn't know what to do in his own home. It was as if someone had been inside and slightly rearranged the furniture. Nothing was obviously changed, but everything was off-kilter enough for him to feel as if someone had come in and touched everything. He felt bereft and indefinitely violated. Without thinking, he went to his date book and when he saw the words *Anna – Dinner* felt an enormous sense of relief. He replayed the message and Anna's voice filled up the room like warm water. Tomorrow was held out to him like an apple. Tomorrow he wouldn't be condemned to be alone in this apartment with the book.

VII

Dolly Holes

He succumbed too easily to her plastic charms, but the lovemaking was paranoid; a clairvoyance cursed the pleasure. A doll maker fucking his marionnette; a common mistake, a common seduction. He pushed at the manufactured edges of her body and it gave here and there in artificial responses. What do you want with a limp child? Unseeing eyes persecuted him for his desire. It's only a doll, he said. It's only a doll, he said again more strongly, feeling the guilt creep in and sully the pleasure. But he couldn't retract his cock from her hole. He was captivated inside the push and pleasure. He was fascinated by the taint and sickness of his hips' motion against the pseudo body. Her only possible response was in the eyes which automatically shut when he laid her down horizontally. He pushed her body upright and the acrylic lids and plastic lashes swept lazily upward. They remained unblinking and focused on his face.

Rebuking him, encouraging him... he could not tell.

He wanted to stop, but his body was driving towards the orgasm like a suicide careening towards pavement. She was sealed with an omniscient squeal, the toy in her throat making squeaking noises when he grabbed her smooth neck and choked. Her mouth was painted in a permanent scarlet O with a little hole there for the bottle. When he finally came, his semen shot in a hot path up the centre of the doll, melting away the plastic as it jetted through her.

At first nothing came out from the centre of the doll, the body sometimes pausing before bleeding as if taking stock of the trauma before letting go with the blood. The precise suspended moment hung between man and doll and then the warm sanguine rush came. Her blue glass eyes, remained undilated, though the plastic lids blinked in shock and a little pain. He wanted to wake, but he was bound to her, cock to dolly hole. He pushed the plastic jointed hips away with as much force as he could, and at last they were separated. Just as he pulled, a human arm shot upward from the centre of the doll wound. The hand was balled into a tight fist. He woke soaked in semen and sweat. When he rolled over, he realised that he had forgotten to put the book away, and it lay there at the foot of the bed. He got up immediately and put it back in the drawer. He slept more fitfully knowing it was locked away.

He started to think that he should get rid of the book. Hoping for some solace in a little science, Lazar dutifully wrote down the dream the next morning and upon looking at the words on the computer screen, he was disgusted at his own obviousness but finally he forgave his unconscious mind its foibles.

He spent the day immersed in the mundane, clinging to the little realities of familiarity even though he knew that fundamentally things were shifting and changing from within. Every now and again he was assaulted by thoughts of the book, and felt exposed and hostile towards the feeling it evoked. He even found himself wishing that he could believe again in the religion of psychiatry, for then he could talk himself out of the compulsion to think about her and the book. He even thought that if he could apply some of the methods he would easily rid himself of the lingering fantasies that were beginning to contaminate his mind via the circuitous route of his soul.

He felt like a child waiting for a special surprise, and the eight o'clock dinner date looked safe yet tantalising on the horizon of his day. He knew he was being ridiculous, but he feared reading the book again. It seemed to appeal to him on a personal level that would not name itself, yet he could not exactly locate where he thought this specific address was emanating from. The only certain sign that he had was that she had selected to leave the book with him, but she could have easily plucked his name from a phone book. She could have selected him as a random participant in some game.

By the close of the day he resolved to take the book to the office with him, to place it in a file and leave it there. He felt some relief in his resolve and went about the business of selecting a wine to take to the dinner party.

VIII

Blind Voyeur

Lazar was accustomed to Jade and Anna's apartment and others like it. He was used to the kind of guests that would accessorise parties such as this. They would all move through the apartment in balletic rounds; a kind of muted dance that is familiar to people accustomed to wealth and abundance. They always struck Lazar as the kind of people used to finding what they expect to find, and shield themselves carefully from messy surprises. Tact and self control was an imperative, as though the influence of money had removed their ability to be brutal. Being rich had removed them from the sphere of common vulgarities such as any overt expression of sexuality. He was used to the stilted flow between people and the oppressive exchanges that filled the time and tasteful space.

He had long ago learned to repress any instinct to analyse others in these situations, for he often found himself in a room at close quarters with so much unspoken despair and impotence that he used to feel as though he might buckle under it all. His marriage had proven that he could not shoulder the responsibility of this kind of empty despair. Lazar denied himself the memory of having any ready tools to decipher their agonies. He always drank too much at parties.

Despite his general dislike of dinner parties, he was very pleased to see Anna and got there early so that he would have time to talk with her before the quiet waltz of boredom began. She greeted him at the door and he felt her warmth immediately. She almost always exuded an internal sun, a calm slow burn that had helped him stay sane through medical school and beyond. Her calm was not maternal or paternal but simply present. She had been a sympathetic pragmatist through his divorce and until recently had been quietly trying to supply him with a new mate. Finally Lazar had told her that he wasn't really looking for "that kind" of relationship, and she had been tactful and smiled.

"Well, honey, when you are, you come to me. I got the goods," she pinched him on the ass to let him know it was OK.

He was grateful that she loved women. Anna was the first lesbian that Lazar had known and her assured self-acceptance and love of her partners had left him feeling impressed and confused as to why he could not feel that way about his own sexuality or his lovers.

"You have to learn to love women like I have, then you'll get it together," she told him one late night over wine.

"How do you love women?" he asked her.

"I love them," she said simply, and he supposed she was right. But women seemed so alien to him. Even after he had been privy to their souls and secrets daily, they still tended to mystify him. Especially when they opened before him on a wave of cool sheeting. Naked and vulnerable.

"Maybe you should try being with a man," she had said and

he laughed too quickly.

"No, Anna. I'm afraid I'm completely heterosexual in my preferences."

"Hmm. Well, in all my years of practice and life, I have yet to meet anyone who was entirely hetero in their preferences. You know I'm right. But I respect your choice."

"It's not a choice. It just is."

"Well, you'll find your way. You will find your way when you least expect it." The way she had said it was filled with such confidence that he nodded like a child following instructions.

He was trying to be patient for the way to reveal itself, but the impatience to escape the feeling of dissatisfaction was unravelling his nerves.

"Hey Simon," Anna greeted him and kissed him. She put her arms around him and hugged him and he sagged against her. He didn't realise until that moment how tense and exhausted the past few days had left him.

"You look a little beat. Come in, have a glass of wine." He followed down the hall.

"Why don't you go say hello to Jade and then come in my room while I finish getting dressed and talk to me." Anna disappeared into the bedroom.

He waited a moment before going in the kitchen. The idea of being alone with Jade made him a little uncomfortable. There was something about her that always left him a little unsettled. When Anna had first started seeing Jade, he had hoped that it wouldn't last, and he didn't know why he had felt that way. Then he realised that what bothered him was her lack of engagement with him. With Anna, with her work. She always seemed slightly false to him. It was nothing overt that she did, it was just his sense about her. Something wrong. Something unresolved and festering. But Anna seemed to be happy with her, and their life together seemed to have fallen into a domestic routine that was cosy.

He found Jade in the kitchen cooking. Her hands were busily flying over the food and her delicate frame amped by an internal buzz.

"Hello Jade," he said and she jumped.

"Jesus! Simon! You scared me." She came over and gave him a dry kiss on the cheek. "How are you?" she said, turning back to her cooking.

"Fine. Good. And you?"

"Nervous as a cat."

"You anxious about this agent?"

"Yes and no. I think it will work out," she said.

"Catherine mentioned St. John once or twice."

Jade turned suddenly. "What did she say?"

"Oh, you know. I can't really remember. But I know he's very influential."

"Yes, he is," she said and went back to her cooking. "We'll see. We've had a number of meetings and he's expressed interest…" Her voice trailed off.

There was something confused about Jade tonight, more so than usual. Lazar wondered if Jade had always had this quality or if he was just noticing it now.

There was an uncomfortable pause and he waited, as he had been trained to do.

"I brought the wine," he said finally.

She turned and said, "Oh, thanks, Simon. Why don't you set it over there. I'm sorry I'm so distracted, I'm just…

That was one of Jade's most recurring lines. "I'm sorry."

"Why don't I go and keep Anna company and get out of your way."

"I'm sorry, Simon. I'll be done in a moment and then we can really visit. OK?"

Lazar was grateful to get away. He sensed trouble and wondered if Jade and Anna had had a fight before he arrived. He flashed back to the few dinner parties that Catherine and he had given when they were trying to salvage their marriage. As if a little dinner party was going to help. He realised that there was probably nothing wrong between Anna and Jade except that they were nervous about their guest. He poured himself a glass of wine from the open bottle on the counter and left the kitchen.

"So what's the big deal about St. John? Catherine mentioned his name once or twice when we were..." He let it trail off. Anna knew the whole story.

He sat down on the edge of the bed, calling into the bathroom where Anna was putting on her make-up. They faced each other through the mirror.

"Yeah. He's this powerful literary agent. I think he'll sign her."

"Have you met him before?"

"No," she said turning and looking at Simon. "But you know I've got a bad feeling about him. I can't tell Jade that, though. But ever since she's been meeting with him she's been ... strange." She turned back to the mirror.

"Strange how?"

"I don't know. Detached. They have these meetings that go on and on. I don't know. It's just weird. I'm just being protective I guess."

"What does Jade think of him?"

"Well, she's not sure. When she comes home from the meetings, I've asked her but she says she's superstitious about talking about it too much until it's a done deal. I guess it's a vibe thing. I don't know." Her voice sounded hard-edged, and Lazar was surprised.

"Ah, vibe. Yeah. That's what I think Catherine said about him."

"Have you talked to her? She called to say hi to Jade the

other day."

Catherine had known Jade from the publishing business, and she had introduced Anna and Jade before she and Lazar had split. Catherine and Jade had maintained a friendly relationship while Anna had stayed quietly neutral for which Lazar was grateful.

"No. I can't talk to her right now. I'm not. . ."

"I know Simon. You don't have to explain. Jade seems to think that if she could get St. John to represent her, it would really help her career. When Jade spoke to Catherine, she agreed."

"It definitely will, but you don't sound too happy about it."

"Oh, no. I am. It's just that I... Yeah, she could really use a boost. The whole freelance journalism thing is getting her down. She wants to do a book and she needs him to do it. So I guess it's good. I don't know where this sense of misgiving is coming from." Anna came out of the bathroom and sat down on the edge of the bed. She took his wine glass and finished what was in it.

"You look tired, Anna."

"I am. Jade and I aren't..." she paused and searched for a succinct way to put it.

"What? Are you having problems?"

"Yeah. We are. But you know I don't really want to talk about it tonight. I want this party to go well for her. How do I look? A haggard old bag?" Anna sat up and checked her reflection in the mirror across the room. There was an unfamiliar insecurity about her tonight. Something about her that he didn't exactly recognise.

"Are you anxious about meeting this guy too?" he asked incredulously. He never associated Anna with nervousness.

"No," she answered quickly. "I just...No, Simon. I just want this party to go well," she said earnestly. "Jade and I have never had a party together, and like I said, things have been a little strained between us lately."

He felt a sudden wave of anxiety himself. He realised that he needed their relationship to be intact. He wanted the security of knowing at least one couple that wasn't falling to pieces.

"Oh, we'll be fine. It's just the usual stuff," she said. She looked at him for a moment. He knew there was something else she wanted to say, but he found himself wanting to close the door before Anna would say it. He didn't want to know if it meant that another relationship was deteriorating.

"Are you sure?" he said against his better judgement.

"No," Anna sighed. The doorbell rang. And they stood there in the bedroom awkwardly staring at each other.

"I'll get it," she said gently.

He suddenly wanted to confess to her about the book. He wanted to tell her about Maya, but something kept him from blurting it out. He wanted to keep Maya to himself for a while. He wondered if that meant that he wasn't going to take the book to the office and lock it away. He pushed the thought out of his mind.

She went to get the door, leaving him in the bedroom alone.

He stayed in the room for a while, feeling the warmth flush his cheeks. He wanted to enjoy the safety of this house for a while. Or at least the illusion of it.

William St. John had a curious way of holding his body. It was as though he were mildly apologetic for having one, and his carriage betrayed a genteel embarrassment. But he was handsome; fragile and handsome. He extended a delicate, white-veined hand to Lazar when they were introduced, and Lazar was surprised by the strength and assurance of St. John's grip. He quickly scanned the man's eyes. They were dark green with yellow specks around the iris and the delicate lift on the outer edges suggested a feline alertness. His lips were full and feminine. He barely smiled and said, "Dr Lazar. Nice to meet you. Doctor of what?"

"I am a psychiatrist." Lazar said.

"Oh, I see." St. John said it as though he were sorry for Lazar. Lazar was more relieved that St. John didn't make any lame joke or pithy quip about shrinks.

"You don't believe in psychiatry?" Lazar asked, more amused than defensive.

"Oh no," St. John said and then moved away to meet someone else. He looked over his shoulder at Lazar for a moment before he was engaged in introduction to someone else. The look left Lazar feeling unsettled. So that's what Jade and Catherine meant by vibe.

There was something unobtrusive but pervasive about St. John's presence in the room. Lazar wanted to venture to guess at some hidden perversity, some dark secret that the man had cleaned up and hidden in some remote part of his brain never to be allowed out. Lazar went and helped himself to another glass of wine and then stationed himself on a couch in a position better to watch St. John work the room.

He was tall but moved with a masculine elegance that some slender men lack. He watched St. John half-smile at Jade and Anna and other guests at the party, and while he seemed charming and was making them laugh in a pleasant low-level hum, there was clearly a part of him that was not engaged in the present. This intrigued Lazar but he also felt a little bit of fearful shame in that he found St. John very attractive. He also found St. John's elusive persona very seductive, from a psychiatric point of view. Lazar rationalised that this made him attractive on a sexual level. He tried to tell himself it was nothing more than force of habit that was colouring his feelings. Yet he felt fairly sure that the man had things to hide. Lazar felt the recently familiar pin of curiosity that seemed to threaten his sense of well-being.

"He's quite good-looking. Jade didn't mention *that*," Anna said quietly in Lazar's ear as she sat down next to him on the couch.

"She probably didn't notice."

"Oh, come on. Even you noticed it."

Lazar turned to Anna. "What do you mean."

"You've been transfixed with him since he came in the house." She laughed and nudged him and then got up to announce dinner.

"Well, I do see what Jade meant by vibe."

"Yeah. He's got that all right," Anna said scrutinising St. John. "But there's something about him that's. . ." Her voice trailed off.

Lazar didn't ask her what she saw. He wanted to find it himself.

Anna seated Lazar next to St. John.

"Are you a voyeur?" St. John turned during dinner and asked Lazar quietly.

"What?"

"Are you a voyeur?"

He asked it in such a sincere and beguiling way that Lazar simply laughed. The dinner conversation hushed and everyone at the table turned politely to wait for Lazar's answer. Even Anna watched him, resting her chin on folded hands.

"I am curious what makes you ask such a question," Lazar replied turning to look at the man. He was so sharp but remained almost voluptuous. His paradoxical sensuality left Lazar unsettled on a basic level that was without familiar language. He pushed the sensation away wilfully.

"I see," was all that St. John said.

There was an annoying patter of laughter from around the table. Lazar noticed that Anna didn't smile, but rather watched St. John in such a way that Lazar knew she was considering him as a psychiatrist rather than a hostess.

St. John wiped his mouth with the white linen and Lazar could swear that he saw his smile pushed into the napkin. He hid it in his lap beneath the table.

Lazar felt exposed and ridiculous. He watched St. John, but the young man's composure was unshaken. He was talking quietly with Jade about some new book that had recently been written about in *The Times*. He felt that St. John's grin was loaded with meaning. He poured another glass of wine and despised himself for his guilt and shame and his irrational tendencies lately. He was beginning to feel superstitious and haunted. He poured enough wine over his feelings to douse them until he got home.

Meeting St. John disturbed Lazar during his entire ride home. He wanted to comfort himself, thinking that the man was a cipher. He tried telling himself that St. John was no more than a self-conscious and affected nothing. But his sensual sensor and the psychiatry that he had been practising for years told him this was not so. St. John seemed metallic and artificial, but there was something peculiarly sincere in his simplicity. Lazar's mind slowly turned inward as if the thoughts were being deflected off the memory of St. John. He wondered whether he was actually less a psychiatrist, having been reduced over the years to nothing more than voyeurism. Was he simply supplying a screen for his patients to project their voices upon? Moreover, was he receiving secret gratification from watching the suffering of others? Did he not take a certain pleasure in their baroque sexual confusions and guilts?

Considering these questions led him to think of Maya. Was he not treading on an ethical borderline in regards to her writings? Technically he wasn't doing anything wrong in reading a journal that a patient had left behind; a patient whose intention was for him to read it. In actuality he wasn't sure of her intention and she wasn't his patient in the traditional sense of the word.

When he reached into his pocket to retrieve his house keys, he also pulled out a business card.

ST. JOHN LITERARY AGENCY

The little card enraged him. He felt violated in the most obscure way. When he stumbled inside his apartment, he immediately threw the card in the garbage and then seconds later withdrew it, wiping the coffee grounds off it. He was still holding the crumpled damp thing when he started towards the bedroom.

Moved by the bluster of drink, and the atavistic disturbance St. John had caused in his body, Lazar stumbled to his bedroom to retrieve the book. He was going to read the whole sordid little thing that night and be done with it, and then he was going to toss the thing in the furnace and burn it. That would assure him a good night's sleep.

When he walked in the room, the book was sitting on the edge of the bed and he was startled enough to stop in his sway and grab hold of the door jam. He could have sworn that he had locked the filthy thing up with the gun the night before. He told himself he was drinking too much.

IX

Bruise Sexy

Maya 3 had that pregnant look that all the men love. Spider-like. Hagborn. Fat with the possibility of poison and web, and she had a stronger will towards violence and chaos than all the previous Maya. She was seeking the confusion rather than tripping over it. She was making the chaos.

Suitors hung around the edges of her skirt in suspense, wanting some of the sick but I walked away from them, feeling foreign inside the feral body. Soon the bleach and sun started weeping internally. I folded inward and when the squalor and noise and light were too burning and too bright, I moved outward between the buildings popping up like wino teeth through the melting streets. I walked in the glamour dream, constricted in the arterial confusion and heat of LA, wandering for days with the withering needles dangling from the crooks in my arms, bootlaces tying me off. This new body was full of disturbances and angles; cracks that etched up my centre, growing and shifting like fault lines. Maya 3 was an earthquake in torn tights and black lipstick, so I put her ass on ice for a while, just enough time to get acquainted with the new shape of the fashionable ferocity.

Bored with the metal, I tore the needles out of my arms like weeds. Something suggested that the body and the dreaming would provide enough pain without. Finally awake, I tacked a map up on the ceiling of my room and spit a tooth east. The incisor landed on Boston. A cruel climate would suit the recently widowed body. It was far away as I could go without falling in the water on the other side. Maya 3 shed the syringic jewellery, untied the tourniquets and left Los Angeles.

I told the cab driver, Kenmore Square and he said, You don't want to go there. That's the asshole of Boston. I said, Yeah. I do. Take me there. He looked at me in the rear view mirror and shook his head.

The place was filled with demented beer boys in oxford shirts and saddle shoes, smiling whitely. Whitely. That white couldn't cushion the ruby red spleen under my tongue and so I lifted the edges of the puritanical asphalt still steaming from the humid summer. I peered just *inside* the asshole of Boston, and there he stood waiting, shining like most murderers do.

He was pointed, his cheeks and nose geniculated in gothic spires jutting atheistically nowhere. He had the mark of the beast on him, a French accent and some kind of hidden disease which caused me to follow him, intoxicated by his belladonna smell and soulless walk. His legs were made of glass, and his fingers too. Maya 3 drew out the seduction like one draws out venom; with tongue and lip.

I trailed him leaving bribes — hints of the crazy whispers under my dress and footprints on his ceiling to show my disregard for gravity. I made subtle suggestions with my hands indicating the huge hole in my middle.

When I could, I slid between the slow flap of his wing and sidling up to his ear I said, tear me open. But his silence was seraphic, the violence in him angelic and pure. My boots were suddenly too heavy and I could not lift off the street to reach to vault where he rested, his back curled against it, black wing folded under the long white arms.

I jumped, heaving the body forward to meet his jagged knuckle and finally he received my skin. At first he only deigned to take a little sip from the razor cut in my leg. The touch of his kiss to my thigh was piercing and it was the first memorable act of willfully induced pain that I conscientiously linked to pleasure. He sent me away with the stitch in my thigh and a small rosebud flowering on my neck. I nurtured the bud with scrupulous vigilance.

Don't come back, he said, wiping his sullied hands and shut himself off with some other willful angel scraped from the sphincter of Boston.

Whore, I called over my shoulder moving down Commonwealth Avenue, the puritans separating and parting to let me by. Along with the first bite of pain, Maya 3 got the first diamond shot of jealousy fired from an elegant gun at close range. I held the tissue and flesh under my skirt. It hadn't made a new wound — only irked the one that already existed.

The lip-made mark on my neck preceded me where I walked, and soon I was becoming the little contusion. The wound in the middle was waking, thirsting for a kill. Certainly there were others who could have done the job, but they would have done it hastily and with some mess. Maya 3 wanted to feel his china sharp body, to thrust her hips over the edges, to throw her face and hands against the brittle grind. She wanted to feel the sensation of dormant pain, to wake the body again and again.

Wasting for him, I dragged myself up hill and stair after him. The need disgusted Maya 3, but she condemned the hunger yet was motivated by it simultaneously.

I need you, she said, over and over to him. To anyone. I need you to. . .

I balked at the implication of the next word. For the first time fear interfered, and it startled the body. The words waited cryogenically on my lip.

Get out, he said, not looking up from his work. She could see his metal exoskeleton pierce the film of his shirt.

No. I need you. I need you to. . . she stammered. It was a mistake to reveal the fear.

He waited, watching her weakness drip on the floor around her shoes and then after a while he attacked. She hurled herself into the contusive kiss — first arms outstretched and diving from his spires — and then covering her breast, she dove from his vault of night sky and slipped into his cold glass sea. The shards of his fingers and knuckle disarranged her lip and cheek.

After the intensity of first impact, Maya 3 drew inward and hung to the crumbling zygomatic arch with broken fingers. The crushing nerve and bone dallied long enough with the erotic so that the imprint was made deep in the muscle memory. The wound creaked and moaned under the stress of birth. The sensation was unbearable and the decaying self sagged against the metallic curvature of the dying body. The new Maya struggled head first from the wound, blind and armless, biting at the umbilicus with strong teeth. But Maya 3 would not give up that easily, even as the blood and afterbirth slid and oozed from mouth and wound.

Yes, the ruined face said. Do it again.

A sweet, high-pitched sigh let itself from the body, a bowed structure reduced to a series of smudges and spittle. He stood over her, his wings flapping in a slow rhythm. He was acutely calm, entirely unmoved by the excesses of his desires. He reached out and dipped his finger in the blood spattering the walls and brought the red-tipped finger to his lip. At the taste of her blood, his wings arced higher than before, the tendons buttressing the leather flap and ligament. A scream of wing made wind, its razor edges strangulating all other sound in the small room.

When he struck her again, her body received the knock-out punch like an annunciation. Blood recoil. Her hips and belly rippled, backfiring and shuddering. Knees folded and bent. The vessels under the skin formed a radiating crown which project- ed silently across her face. The impact shook any last memento of sentimentality from the erotic. His fist forced the erotic into a new body, a tight-laced and cruel skin. The feelings of plea- sure and fear were welded together in a tenacious marriage.

She fell into a stupor and hardly recognised the shapes of the other body as it entered the room.

What did you do? another man said.

I…she heard the murderer giggle.

He had suddenly acquired the girlish laugh of a demented nun. She tried to get up, but could not. The ache kept her crucified on the wooden floor, but her good eye stayed open as she watched the two figures move around her body.

What have you done to her, the other voice insisted.

Awestruck shame entered the room.

I got carried away, he said. The quality of uncertainty in his voice pleased her.

No shit, you asshole. She looks dead.

A foot nudged the body of Maya 3.

Someone's going to call the cops, you stupid fucker. Why did you have to go and do that again? I told you to stay away from girls. You know how you get. You stupid fucker.

There was a sound of skin meeting palm. A mere slap across the face.

No, wait, her murderer said. He reached out and grabbed the other voice. Maya 4 lifted herself on busted arm and watched the two boys kiss. She laughed. She was waking up to the circus of sex. Boy boy fist fuck. Never knew it could happen that way. She watched their contortions of sex from inside her muted bubble of injury. They were fucking each other over her dead body. The irony was not lost.

Eventually some cops and a state technician came to collect the gin-soaked heap of skin that was the shell of Maya 3. They tried to revive her with whiskey and sutures, but Maya 4 already had her claws dug deep into this world.

I'm dead, I said.

No, honey. You've been hurt that's all.

I'm dead, I said.

She's in shock. Someone get her a drink to calm her down.

Yeah, she said. Give me a shot of that whiskey and close the wound with paper staples. It'll be reopened soon enough. As soon as I find an appropriate surgeon for the job.

Yeah, OK, the technicians said and left her alone.

Her wrecked face and broken-down body left the technicians wondering what the crazy bitch had to do to get a beating like that.

When he impacted his body against mine in that way, the course was set. The Via Negativa was permanently etched inward and out. The scar over my eye is the brand. The scar in my eye is the lesson. Pain is growth. Love is death of the self. Love is death and rebirth through enforced suffering.

Suffering was reinformed and alleviated heaving us towards better, newer, more entertaining schemes of torture. Reinforced suffering would bring about the liberation of Maya 30.

❖❖❖❖

He was brutalised by this naked admission of the birth of the sadomasochistic cycle. He had certainly treated sadists and masochists in every different manifestation. From those who felt the need to act it out esoterically — the theatre of leather, the whips, the threats and dramatic humiliations, or those who acted it out in the subtle power manipulations and tortures of withholding and lying. He had at times been fascinated with the symbolism that he had given his patients actions, but she was writing it for him, and it was phenomenally grotesque to watch unfold. He was seeing a garden of red jewel-like organs spill out over the white thigh, glistening against her pale skin as he gazed upward through her cunt.

The sensation pleased him, her words arousing him in a way that he felt was slightly unbecoming or disgraceful. He wanted to find her and fuck her and he didn't want the feelings to stop. The torque of her words and the vector of the book on his lap was contaminating him in a way that was almost pleasant. He felt like a host to her fever dream and language virus and he knew that this amorphous disease was the closest he was going to get to fucking her.

He decided to keep the book a while longer. He shoved St. John's card in the page where he'd left off reading and staggered to the dresser that had become her hiding place.

X

Body Mirror

What have you done to her? He turned and found St. John standing close enough so that the whisper of his breath excited the timid nerves around the base of his spinal chord.

I guess I got carried away, he replied quietly. I wanted to watch her...

He looked down and there was blood on his hands. The two men stood alone in the stark room. Industrial steel indicating that it was probably institutional. It smelled like a hospital.

I knew you had it in you, St. John said and moved even closer.

Lazar meant to keep him away but St. John smiled grimly and said, I knew you weren't just a voyeur. He reached out and put his fingertip on Lazar's lip and pulled the trigger.

Lazar woke with an erection.

When he tried to masturbate, St. John seemed to leak into

his imagination. With some embarrassed hesitance, Lazar gave into the sexual ire that St. John had ignited in him. He unveiled that sleeping part of his psyche. He felt ridiculous at his own sense of shame and awkwardness in fantasising about a beautiful young man. Yet it had been years since he had felt any kind of erotic charge from another man, and he never remembered it feeling quite this earnest.

Angry at the insistence of the imagination, he spat on his hand and pulled his cock hard at the root. The first stage of relief torched a blue flame river up through his middle. Closing his fist around his shaft, he felt the sameness of St. John's body, and the sameness turned to a kind of kinship, a oneness that he didn't understand or want. He tried to pull away from the sensation, but he had already let St. John enter a sphere that he usually reserved for the soft plush of women's hips and breasts. But the tectonic push and pull of muscle to muscle was mean-edged and exciting. He pulled at his own body harder and harder, wanting the sensation to hurt him into satisfaction. He wanted the hurting to wake him, to dull the fantasy into submission by killing it. By coming. But the lingering image of St. John's angular face and feline eyes probed into his body in a way that no one had done recently. No one, except of course a fictitious woman.

He suddenly stopped. He sat up, his cock and hand weak from the mild battering.

He realised that Maya and St. John had a very similar smell.

Lazar toiled under the burden of appearing caring, but his clinical demeanour was slipping. He noticed the hurt glances of at least three of his patients which was an indicator to him that they knew he wasn't paying attention to what they were saying. He used to be more vigilant about changing his face for the occasion, but he was too confused.

He started to think that he should probably take some time off, but the thought of having nothing to do but read that book frightened him much more than the threat of malpractice. He felt caged and alone.

When he got home, he phoned Anna.

"I don't like him," she said flatly.

"Who," Lazar said, pouring his first drink, of course knowing who she was referring to.

"St. John," she said with finality.

"Why?"

"There's a hidden agenda in there underneath that lovely facade. I think you know what I mean. Jade is angry with me. She thinks I'm not being supportive."

"Does he want to represent her."

Anna sighed. "Oh, Christ I don't know. But you know, Simon, for the first time in years I'm actually a little jealous. He's all Jade's been talking about for weeks, and now that I've met him, I can see why. And I don't like it."

"You don't think she's attracted to him. That's ridiculous. Jade is… "

"She is."

"No, you're making it up."

"No. I'm not. He's one of those people that everyone wants to fuck."

Lazar downed the rest of his drink.

"What do you think his pathology is?"

"I don't think he's got one. That's his problem."

Lazar suddenly wanted to tell Anna about the book, but he knew he couldn't until he read a couple more chapters. At least one more.

"What did you think of him?" she asked earnestly.

"I haven't thought of him at all," he replied.

He had been the banisher of secrets for so long, he forgot about the intrinsic power and pleasure that was at their core. It made him feel excited and nauseous.

When he called one of the women that he fucked on nights like this, he felt like a traitor. He just didn't know who he was betraying anymore.

XI

Snapshot Raphael

Maya 4 had a pathetic fuck me beat me bitch perfume that choked out the cigarette and piss smells of the Rat on Commonwealth Avenue. A face like mine was a siren and the wound unsutured from the last suicide was weeping, red tears staining my shirts and dripping around my shoes.

Looking like I did, it didn't take long for the killer to find me. He swiped the life out of Maya 4 in a matter of one thirty-fifth of a second. Maya 4 was a goner before she was even upright and walking. The suicides were getting considerably cheaper with every fuck.

He wanted to take my picture. I told him it would give me too much soul to have my image captured on a ghost plate like a negative, and I don't want a soul, baby. I just want you to fuck me dead. Harder dead. Deader than before. Deader than dead. Deader than a fucking crucifixion nail.

He laughed.

You think I'm joking. I offered my wrists for the cuffs. For the razor, for the butt, for the kiss.

He pushed the curtains of smoke aside, his barbed wire nimbus poking the softer parts of my breast and neck. I watched the blood mix with the cut in the centre. I looked inward and saw the shining teeth of a new Maya. Silver-shaped fangs. I grew closer to becoming my cunt with every kill.

He lifted me by the heel of my boot and dragged me down the streets, my ass and back sliding along the ice-covered roads. I looked up at the tips of the buildings shapeless and grey against the close night sky. When I opened my mouth the whole cup of wine inside the Big Dipper washed down my throat, and I gagged and vomited useless devils of vitriol. There were strong little demons that kicked and angered the edges of my pussy and wound. I thought my body wouldn't contain just one wound or just one devil. And there's always room for one more sin.

Open me up.

When he kissed me, I flinched and the blood dribbled down our chins. The crooked edges of my cut lips busted open again, still sore from the last suicide.

What the hell happened to you?

I got fucked.

Yeah. I can see that. Who did that to you. I'll kill him. He wasn't talking to me. He was talking to his gun and film. His testosterone soliloquies were all right. They distracted me from the nausea. The balsam black from the sky's cough syrup was sickening. I wondered what it would be like to vomit while getting fucked and thought it was a distinct possibility. We got to a house and he picked up my limp body and trudged up the stairs, as if fucking me was turning into a chore. The rooms were filled with a stifling warmth, old water heaters indiscriminately spreading heat. Like me. A beat me fuck me bitch.

Your black eye turns me on, he said. It looks wicked sick. Come here.

I couldn't see anything in the hot room but the body. When I pulled the brown shirt and the swastikas away, I found the evidence on his wrist. I put my mouth over the vertical scars.

Botched it, I said.

Bitch, he said, but was too drunk to do anything other than fuck my mouth shut. She opened my throat to his thick cock, feeling the head snake down the palate, a warm wrinkle of flesh against her chin. Maya 4 split into a confused series of fragmented sensations. The oxygen was pushed down and away from her, but at the same time a rush of energy and power shot up through the middle of the wound. The centre. Her mouth was making him hold her close. He cupped her head roughly between his thighs, and she rested her hands on either leg, her arms raising like an insect, her fingers digging into the cut muscle. Her back bones jutted like truncated bug wings. His physical strength was crushing, and she thought at first the suicide would be quick and chaotic, like a photograph. A gunshot. But he pushed her head in varying strokes, making her tongue and lip meet the shiver and rhyme of his body. She recreated both of them with her mouth, and he was doing the same with his hands and cock. He pulled her up abruptly.

I want to come in you, he said and put his mouth on hers.

He licked the cuts on her lips, biting them, needling them with the edges of his teeth. And then he lifted her like she was a small rock and pounded her down over his body, splitting the wound right open and the new Maya rolled out like a smaller stone. She was still in the foetal embrace, the suicide not yet complete.

As he manipulated her body around the strong contours of his cock, his mouth and her wound connected. Maya 5 slow-

ly opened her eyes, seeing only edges of skin and bone ignited by sweat. There was no room beyond the edges of his
abdomen cutting into the V of his pelvis and then further into
the wound where he had gone inside to die with Maya 4.
Finally with a low howl, he came and vanished.

While he slept, she touched the body in the darkness, able
to search it like a scientist because she didn't know him. She
didn't want to know him in any other way than the braille of
a one-night stand.

Day didn't seem to visit the room and Maya 5 waited there,
curled up under the dead weight of the arm for a long time.
Finally, strong enough to be upright, she yanked her spine
upward, pulling herself vertebrae by vertebrae towards the
edge of the bed looking for a match to light her cigarette.

When she struck the match, the room was briefly illumi-
nated. The shriek surprised her before she could stifle it, but
it did not wake him. She dropped the match and then when
she felt composed enough, she lit another. His windowless
room was covered entirely — ceiling, floor, walls, door, and
windows with black and white photographs, photocopies and
vivisected magazine pictures. Images of emaciated bodies were
piled high against his closet. At one end of the bed there were
pictures of empty socketed and decapitated children. The
holes gaped stupidly. The entire ceiling of the room was an
expanse of skin opening like an overripe fruit. Pictures of
napalm fires, cities in riot, photographs of anarchic starvation
punctuated the pattern of singular bodies in pain. His bedroom was an altar to Armageddon and she smiled at the poet-
ry of having committed such a senseless act of violence under
all these gloriously stolen moments.

I gathered my clothes in my arms and carried them out on
to the street. Dressing in the snow, I realised that I would have

to leave Boston soon because the trail of murders could clearly be traced to me in all this cold white. I dressed the wound under a street lamp somewhere near Roxbury and started back home through the snow, the trail of ink showing up starkly on the snow.

Even though it was still dark, the four o'clock moon was too bright for the foetal eyes of Maya 5, and so pulling the skin shut and the hood over my head, I bent forward and headed deeper into the hollow pit of mourning.

XII

Accidental Annulment

He felt sick. He had hurt her. She lay stricken and coiled at the edge of the bed for a while and he found himself studying the marks on her back and ass. He found himself thinking that he could have done more and still not seriously injured her. He wondered at the simultaneous fragility and resilience of the body.

What am I going to tell my husband about these? she said following his gaze to the marks on her arms.

She looked up at him, half proud, half accusing.

Tell him to go to hell, he said taking his eyes off the reddening skin.

Now that it pleased her, it ruined his fascination with them. She was perceiving the marks as some sort of melodramatic fuck scene, while he was witnessing a latent feature of his sexual personality in the process of being born.

Yes, you're right, she said getting up uneasily.

He thought that the bruises didn't become her. She was too

far away from understanding the beauty of animals and their reasons. She was too far away from the passion that was at the heart of the welts' delivery.

But if I left him, our sex life would probably die.

She was right and he was surprised at her insight. She went towards the bathroom, but paused by the dresser and rested her hand on the edge.

Lazar wanted to tell her to get away from it, feeling jealously protective. She waited by the dresser for a moment just watching him.

I'm not as much of an idiot as you think, she said, going into the bathroom. I know there's someone else, she said, not turning back to face him.

Yes, he said. There is.

She didn't respond.

He knew it was dangerous to let her go away angry because like all of them, she carried with her a weapon. She was after all still technically under his medical care. It could ruin his practice and when he considered it seriously, he found he did not care.

Are you sure that's what you want? she said, coming back out of the bathroom, her breasts securely strapped in and her ass and pussy shielded. She obviously felt she had more ammunition when her sex was covered up.

Yes.

She raised her eyebrow and cocked her hip in a way that suggested blackmail. He didn't move, knowing her psychological patterns well enough to know that she wouldn't ultimately have the stamina to ruin him.

OK, Simon. If you think that's what's best.

He was relieved to see another one go for the last time.

For the next few days, he left the book in the drawer. He didn't dream, but his sleep was restless and empty. His practice was slipping, and he found himself growing compulsively hopeful about Maya's return.

When he went home from the office, he poured himself drinks enough to self-medicate and then he wandered around the apartment, careening off various pieces of furniture. It was as if he suddenly didn't know what to do with his body. His mind was preoccupied with their next meeting. How had she changed? How she would change?

He found himself lost in projections that focused on her. Was she wandering the city, laughing her hideously malformed giggle into a black glove? Was she seeking a new lover to devour under her suicidal cunt?

He never had really understood the gospel of addicts. He had listened to countless stories of mad-driven love towards women, men, booze, coke. But now their stories were coming back to him in slips and fragments of a lethargic pain that would not rid itself.

Just as he finally readied to break the spell and confess to Anna about the book, she phoned.

"Simon. He's signed Jade," she said. There was an edge in her voice that was unrecognisable. Now he knew how Anna's fear sounded and he liked it.

"I'm so glad you called," he said into the phone.

"She's having dinner with him tomorrow night. Will you go out with me? I need to be with a friend."

His confession had been annulled by fate.

"I'll pick you up at eight."

St. John hung around their table like Dracula; present everywhere but unseen and virtually unknowable. Lazar was surprised when he picked Anna up because it seemed as if St.

John's recent presence in their life had drained some of her sun, and she looked wan and older.

"I know I'm being ridiculous," she said to him as they sat down to dinner. "But I have such a bad feeling about him. It's not based on anything tangible, and that's what's driving me crazy. I can't figure out what kind of perverse projection I'm throwing on him. But whatever it is, it isn't good. I know you know what I'm talking about. I saw your reaction to him at dinner last week."

He wanted to tell her that she was misinterpreting his reaction to St. John, but he didn't honestly know what his feelings about the strange man were. He thought about the business card shoved inside Maya's book. He thought of the book and their similar smells. Maya and St. John. Violence.

"I don't think you have to worry." He didn't know why he was lying to her, but it felt devious and good. Anna looked at him earnestly and for a moment it pierced his psyche because he knew he was inadvertently hurting her.

"I want to believe you, but there is something that I'm picking up intuitively about him that's dangerous."

"Dangerous in what way? Manipulative? Dishonest?"

"No. It's not that simple. Manipulative yes, but in a really deviant way. I've had patients like him before and they've always caused a similar reaction in me."

"Which is?"

"Disgust."

Of course, he too felt a lingering feeling about the man that was confused and somewhat, but not entirely negative. But he was starting to fear revealing his thoughts regarding St. John, as if bringing them to the surface would dismantle the driving sensual confusion.

"Are you afraid of him?" he asked Anna.

"No!" she exclaimed too quickly. "Yes. . ." she ran her hands through her shining black hair. "I'm afraid for Jade. I'm afraid for us. Oh Christ, I don't know."

"What do you think is going to happen?"

"Oh, I don't know, Simon," she said and Lazar felt himself slipping away. He didn't want to help her. He didn't want to help himself, he wanted to go towards the place that she was trying to pull away from.

He made more feeble attempts to alleviate Anna's anxiety and then cut the dinner shorter than usual. At first he declined to go up for a nightcap.

"Don't you want to hear how Jade's night went with him?" Anna said, pleading a little. He had never seen this side of her in all the years he had known her and it vaguely pleased him that she wasn't immune to the natural disasters of being human.

The subtextual mention of St. John, the promise that he might get greater insight into the man's motivations regarding Jade or anything, drove Lazar upstairs for a drink even though he wanted to get away from Anna. She was becoming a milestone; an indicator for what Lazar once was and what he was moving past. She was health and wanted to move into disease. He agreed to go upstairs.

Jade wasn't home yet. Four drinks later and the hour nearing four, Lazar bid farewell to his distraught friend.

"Anna, don't worry. I'm sure you'll work it out with her."

Anna simply stared at him a little dead-eyed. She had already withdrawn into her own machinations about her lover's apparent infidelity.

XIII

The Catherine Wheel

He was surprised that any dream could cut through all the wine and brandy he had consumed with Anna the night before. But it had burned through his unconscious like a controlled fire. Pointed. Necessary. Destructive. It was the noise in his dream that was immediately memorable; there was so much screaming. So much applause.

He wasn't prone to recurring dreams, at least not that he could remember vividly. But the twins visited his unconscious mind for the second time, and even inside the reason of sleep, he found himself surprised and pleased to see them again. He felt a very real sense of opportunity; as if this time he would know what he was supposed to do to them.

In his dream he found himself entering a small dark room. The air was close and warm. It smelled like faeces and sweat. Musky. The odour of near-death. Iron gears shifted and groaned.

The twins were before him, naked, bald and still joined just above the waist. The abnormal continuation of their skin aroused him as it had before, and he stared at it for an extended time. He felt his body temperature change, and the tingling of blood rushing to his cock did not surprise him. He felt that they belonged there. They were bound to a large wheel that was clearly recognisable as a mechanism of torture. A Catherine Wheel. Their centre of gravity was displaced and they hung in a web of leather strapping and wooden spoke. Their jointed bodies formed the hub of the wheel, their legs and arms spread so that their cunts were opening slightly and their breasts were pulled taut across the sternum. The circles of their aureoles formed another hub within the wheel.

He was fascinated and aroused by her helplessness and by the disjointed sensation that he was somehow responsible for her position. There were familiar patterns of welts and fingerprints on the girl's tights, very similar to the ones that he had left on his former lover some nights before. He felt in his dream, that he had made the marks on the twins, and the thought pleased him. The fact that their faces were emotionless bothered him though and he found that he wanted to see them weep. He wanted to pull the pain out of them audibly and visibly, and this sensation was much stronger than the urge to fuck either of them.

He wanted her to tell him.

Tell me, he said.

I already have, the girls replied. They spoke as one.

Another man stood in the corner. He was shrouded by shadows but his laughter rang through the stinking chamber.

He turned towards the source of the laughter and was slightly bothered by the fact that the man was obscured by the darkness. He felt his attention being divided between the desire to extract something from the freakish twins and to see the man who stood just out of sight. He found the divisive pull of his desires unbearable and so he forced his gaze away from the corner.

Maya, he said carefully.

It was more a question than an address. One of the twins turned her head towards him while the other remained staring at the ceiling. He looked up and saw an enormous Mitsubishi monitor. There was a crowd gathered watching. There was smoke behind the enormous audience. Pyres. None of the scene seemed foreign. The whole room, the crowd, the man in the corner all seemed to be a natural turn of events.

The twins watched him calmly without speaking. He felt frustrated that he was not inspiring more fear in them. More pain. He knew he was responsible for her situation and it pleased him, but he still felt that she kept a secret and he wanted it. He wouldn't feel satisfied until he was freed from the absurd domination of her passive smile. It enraged him that she could control him from her position on the wheel. Maya, he said again.

Yes, father, she replied.

I will hear your confession now.

I have already confessed, she replied, her gaze not wavering from his.

He nodded to the man in the shadows, accepting that the stranger was an accomplice in some way that he did not fully comprehend. The wheel turned and the crowd cheered. Lazar looked up at the screen on the ceiling. The eager faces from the broadcast watched the torture expectantly. He hated the vulgar carnivorous hunger of the masses, but he hated her composure more. As the wheel turned the stretch of skin that connected them was pulled. It looked extremely painful and this pleased Lazar.

Stop, he ordered the man when the twins were upside down before him.

I want to know your secrets, he said to them. I want to know. You already know.

He stepped up on the platform that was constructed to hold the wheel. Tell me, he shouted. Tell me.

I already have, said the twins still not looking at him.

Before he knew what was happening, he had taken his cock out and shoved it towards one of the girl's mouth. He did not feel of his body so much as a series of angles and motions attached to a penis. When he tried to shove his cock into her mouth, he found that her jaw was locked in a tetanal grimace and he reached down and put his fingers on her lips, prying her mouth open. A scroll of paper was inside her palate instead of a tongue and it rolled out over her eyes and forehead. He read the words.

The period at the end of the last sentence is the good bullet.

Her lips suddenly opened so wide that the jaw effortlessly separated from its hinges. The cracking of bone and tearing of skin was a sound louder than the wheel. The girl split wide down the middle and he felt his whole body lunge forward as if driven into the wet visceral mess. The warm wound cleaved and swallowed his pelvis. The crowd outside cheered.

I said, stop the wheel, Lazar shouted as he was pulled into her quicksand. He wanted more but he felt panicked that he would kill her before he got the words out of her, even if the object of his desire was uncertain. He felt sure that he would know it when it presented itself.

I have, said the man calmly. He was still shrouded in shadows.

Lazar woke up.

The dream stayed with him through the day, bothering him. Fragments appeared vividly in his psyche and confronted his body, even as he tried to listen to his patients' drone. He found that he was less disturbed by the dream than the others even though the physical memory was almost frightening. He was coming to feel that the dreams were a natural manifestation of his waking life and felt increasingly teased by the contact with Maya through his unconscious. The anxious feeling of having met her again in such circumstances was not altogether unpleasant, nor was it a good feeling. It was diseased, compelling. Sexy.

I feel as though you're not listening to me, she said.

He looked at his patient as she sat in the leather chair across from him, looking wounded and pathetic.

I'm not.

After she left he told his receptionist to call all his patients and tell them that an emergency had arisen and that he was not going to be available for consultation for the next two weeks.

The secretary was scrupulously unemotional. Is there anything I can do to help? she said, not really meaning it.

No, Lazar answered. Just tell them to call the alternative number provided. Use Keating as my replacement. I'll call him.

There's going to be some problems, she said. I can tell you that now.

I don't care, he said. I don't care. His face must have shown the breaking.

She nodded and started filing through the Rolodex.

He went back into his office and grabbed the laptop computer. He locked his files and turned out the lights. He said to the secretary as he was going. Forward all emergency calls to Dr Keating.

She nodded.

I don't want to be paged, he said.

But what if —

Tell them to call Keating. I've got to go.

He felt the edges of his body sharpen towards desperation. He had to get out of the office immediately. I've got to go.

She nodded again, avoiding looking at his face as if his expression might be contagious.

I will check in with you in a few days, he said.

Walking through the doors of the building, he knew he had started the process of liberating himself from the pain by heading straight towards the wound.

XIV

Paper, Scissors, Rock

Maya 5 was an unreliable hand-gun. She ran herself listlessly into the oncoming man like simple prey. Maya 5 was born bored and gave way to Maya 6 easily as a wind defying ballistic tip entering the fragile cavity of skin and bone. Their white bullets had maximum long range efficiency and the suicide opened to the ballistic tip ammo because of its absolute accuracy and violent expansion.

The next cycle of suicides were fired off quickly, without thought or memory of their mechanism. I received their unforgettable rounds through her steel barrels. I died, she was born. She died, I was born. She remained a gun. The suicides were speedloaders, varying only in bullet styles. None of the murders were clean, though they were exceptionally quick. Forgettably painless.

The slow and tortured deaths were the only ones that entertained me. It is the same now as then. I wait impatiently in this hotel for the last, writing away my existence. With every eulogy for the Maya suicides, the body looses its deformed definition and heavy-boned armature.

The next Maya moved too quickly and gracelessly through the metal of hip to hip contact to remember incidentals. The body left on those beds was the *corpus delicti*; the only indicator that the suicide had actually happened. These stupefied Maya flew from the corrupted scenes. Seeking another and then another, seeking the suicide moment with the alacrity of a junky. Unburned powder stuck in her pubic hair and around the edges of her cunt. Vague proof some sex had happened in the middle of all the murder and mayhem.

The men and Maya were like cans on a fence. Ragged NRA targets flown between apartments and crashing cars. Seas of booze and sloppy sideways kisses. Transatlantic plane rides and finally a ticket back to the overexposed streets of LA.

The arrested development of the suicides in the next five Maya were the result of fouling, incompatible ammunition, timing problems and poor tolerances. After all, the modern double-day revolver's design has certain tight tolerances and inherent vulnerabilities that are conducive to malfunctions. Even so, the revolver is still the better choice (over the auto pistol) for anyone who is not a hardcore gun enthusiast.

Yes, there were some minor chambering problems: bullets jumped their crimp and crept forward under recoil and tied up her cylinder rotation. Somewhere between the death of Maya 4 and the birth of Maya 10, I found that hand-loads were not a good idea. Opt for the factory-loaded boys, she said.

Compatible ammunition…though it is said that factory loads fire on the warm side and the extensive shooting of very hot loads will of course accelerate wear and eventually cause mechanical problems. This may compromise reliability.

Maya 10 was born a cool .357 SIG, one of the finest defensive rounds to be had. She was much more pleasant to shoot than any of the revolvers — I had the capacity, compactness and speed of reloading inherent in the design, and I was out-fitted with 125 grain full-metal jacket flat nose ammo, a naughty 15 round magazine, and special short trigger so that it would be easier for him to get his fingers in the right spot. Black Teflon silencer absorbing light and sound

Maya 10 was born with great sights and a delightful trigger pull, and she fit into his hand like she was made for him. She had learned that he great majority of gun failures were either the result of dirty corroded guns; incompatible ammunition; or combinations thereof.

Don't unnecessarily fuck with the factory integrity of the gun, Maya 10 said to her suicide trick and he nodded in silent agreement.

The hollow points delivered good accuracy and came out of me like liquid. Wet, smooth. Easy. Not the kind of recoil I used to get in revolvers. Maya 10 was a good match for the next suicide.

I could hear his car before I saw him, and the muscle sound of the old V8 let me know that he was the next bleak angel that would deliver the Maya.

His white car screamed to a rubber-fried halt in front of the Atomic Cafe on First, and he slid the heavy chain from his neck, swinging it over his head like a steel-linked lassoo. He felled a young cholo in a hairnet and he thought that East LA was his prize that night. He stood over the bloodied body of the kid thinking he was noble as Cassius Clay winning the heavyweight title. I stood on the other side of the street which was still officially Little Tokyo. We sized each other up across the river of cooling asphalt and broken yellow lines. He swung his bloodied chain overhead again, and I was hypnotised by it's whir and whistle cutting up the dry night. I crossed the river.

Here she come, he sang. Just a walkin' down the street.

I marched towards him, my double-action heels digging into the asphalt, injuring the streets. His lip lifted and his chrome teeth caught the halogen light and threw it back at me, cutting me above my right eye. It left a little scar running over my brow, the blood burning a blue-green tear. As I got closer, I knew he could get the job done even if he was just a grubby little .22.

If you hold a small bore gun close enough, and at just the right angle, they still have some stopping power. A .22 would bring the suicide out in a low-budget pop.

Paper, scissors, rock; he said and squared his hips for a shoot-out.

Paper covers rock, I said, moving closer so I could smell him. Scissors cut paper. He smelled like diesel fuel. Rock smashes scissors, I said, through my teeth. He smelled of steroids and gun oil.

He said don't fuck with the factory integrity of the gun.

I can give you lighter, smoother, more limber trigger action, baby.

Jomé baby, Jomé.

He laughed and got in the car. The V8 purred and growled rearranging my ribs and hair. His teeth clacked when he laughed and the sound slid out of his steel barrel like extra lube. He drove away leaving a grease spot and me there on First and Alameda. I was drawn, my game ready. Maya 11 was already pushing the slide back and nudging the edges of the wound with her bare hands and I couldn't stop the turning of a trick birth mid-labour.

The seduction of two killing machines is a hardened, chrome waltz; the bodies don't hold, but slide and grate against one another in brief spates of feeding frenzies. He drove back around down First street where I stood waiting. I just wanted to fuck with you a little, he said laughing, throwing the door open. A gauntlet.

I knew you would come, I said.

Just get your fat ass in.

My ass ain't that fat, I said climbing into his trap.

Baby, a woman without ass is a woman without soul. You got a big dark juicy soul. He squeezed the flesh under my black sex leaving a purple grape bruise. His fingers grazed the skin looking for the star-shaped entry point.

We drove through the East LA streets, cutting through the mini-mall parking lots, the creepy night day of LA illuminating sweating gang bangers, bandits and Bloods. Cutting across towards downtown, he ran over Indian winos and boracchito lining 7th. He kept his finger on my trigger and one hand on the wheel. When he stopped the car and leaned over he pushed his mouth over mine. My tongue slid over his smooth steel teeth and then I bit his lower lip hard. He grabbed my hair and tried to pull me off his mouth, but I would not let go and our first kiss turned into a Mexican stand off. We remained drawn and cocked, lip-locked and tangled as we struggled upstairs. We were distracted by the duel, bothered by the interference of the bullet proof t-shirts, combat boots, Kevlar underwear. When we were finally stripped of any protective gear, we cautiously moved around each other's angles and holes, never removing our laser sights from the chest. The weapons were never lowered during in the fray. Simple necessities of the fuck.

I studied his skin with my scope. He was smooth and golden, interrupted in places with puckered scars and hand-poked tattoos made with needle thread and India ink. I reached down and tickled the area between his extractor star and the cylinder and he said, basé me.

Liquidate me, I said.

Paper covers rock. Rock smashes scissors.

Gun shoots gun, Maya 10 said, hardly out of her holster.

Maya 11 pulled back the edges of the wound like an automatic slide, the hole inside itching to impact with the dying. His ejector rod was tight and his screws properly fastened. He moved well for a .22, but was no match for a .357 SIG.

You must be some kind of slut bitch to know so much about guns, he said, pushing his barrel into mine.

I am, I said. I'm a whore. All guns are whores. I thrust my body forward with every foot-pound I had in me. I pushed my tits out to meet the impact.

Are you saying I fuck whores, you bitch? He pulled back.

Maya 10 knew she was going to have to piss him off enough so that he'd kill her.

Yes, I said. Don't stop. Fuck me, slay me. Exterminate this desire.

His cock expanded violently inside the metal shaft of my cunt. The danger in the room gave off a burnt smell.

People have died for less, he said, fucking her harder.

He pulled her off him, and shoving her to her knees, holding his cock to her temple. Loaded. Ready. Fire. How's it feel to be so near death, whore? People have died for less.

Maya 10 laughed. Fuck you, she said.

Maya 11 emerged one-handed from the wound. Fuck you, you mother-fucking wet-back turd, shouted Maya 10. She closed her eyes tight waiting for the bliss of the bullet entrance. The pause was unbearable. He withdrew, reeling off her body like a ricocheted miss.

Pussy, she spat contemptuously and started to reholster her cunt. Misfire.

He grabbed her and holding her by the flesh on the back of her neck, drew his cold-cocked prick across her throat. A trickle of blood cut a warm bath down her middle and was subsumed into the wound.

You're a coward. You're a fucking coward with worn-out

ratchet teeth and a weak cylinder bolt. Chinga su madre. Chinga su madre, she said over and over, the words bubbling over the fear and blood from her slit throat.

He pushed her against the wood chair and held the arms down so hard they cracked off. She waited for the bullet again. Chinga su madre, she said again and again as he staggered drunkenly away.

Hey man, what do I have to do to get you to fuck me? She yelled, swinging the broken armchairs at him.

Rock smashes scissors, he said, careening towards her double-barrelled breasts.

Violence begets violence, she said, opening her mouth and putting her lips around the cool barrel. Her teeth knocked against the tempered chrome and he pushed the revolver further into her body until it jabbed and pushed out the wound.

The appearance of the new Maya were increasingly seamless from being to non-being to being again. Effortless. A trigger pull. Pow. Maya 10 was dead.

Misfire. Timing problems. She took her mouth from the gun and laughed. Laughter is the best weapon.

He shoved his .22 in the hole in her neck and shot her.

Fuck you, he said again and again, firing the whole round in the chamber. People have died for less. People have died for less. He jammed his cock further down her busted gun. He reloaded and fired until she was just a hole-bitten corpse hanging off the tip of his cock. His body shuddered from the recoil and kick of his little .22. The bed was covered with insults and blood. While he rested, his mouth open, the dead gun lying on his chest over a tattoo of the Virgin of Guadeloupe, Maya 11 came out from under cover.

Once the piece has been fired, the slide has to be driven back with sufficient force so that the extractor can clear the empty chamber. When it kicks, it is clear of the ejection port.

The slide then drives another round into the chamber to continue the cycle.

Maya 11 dragged the old carcass of Maya 10 to the corner of East 6th and left the skin there in a pool of weary light. The cholos would clean the body in the night, taking with them the skeleton shape of the .357.

Maya 11 strapped on her shoes and clicked down the street, looking for a rumour of peace.

XV

Snuff

he uncanny choice of Maya's chosen metaphor left him paralysed with a numb paranoia.

A .357

He had chosen the gun because it was known for its smooth handle. It was true what she had written: the bullets slide from the SIG like violent liquid. Unlike a revolver, the .357 SIG was a gun that didn't want to jump out of your hand.

He realised, as he set the book away from his body, that he was starting to entertain faint delusions that the book was accommodating him in calculating way. He thought about Heisenberg's Principle of Uncertainty. As in any experiment, the book seemed to be effected as much by his interaction with it as it was with him. These transformations in the object of experimentation, he knew, could change in ways ranging from the subtle to the profound. Yet resorting to science left him feeling empty and uneasy. It was no longer a rock which he chose to cling to. He set himself adrift in the chaos. He didn't know whether he had just elected to let the book affect him in such a critical and confusing way, but as he examined his feelings, he found he didn't particularly care about himself. He only wanted to get closer to Maya. Willpower had kept him from simply flipping to the end of the book to find out where she was leading him. He recognised that as a cheat, and for the first time in many years, Lazar didn't want to cheat.

He searched his mind weakly attempting to latch on to a realistic thread. No one knew about the purchase of the gun…except for one of his former patients. Not even his ex-wife knew about his recent fascination with firearms. He couldn't even really explain it to himself.

One day, a sense of blandness had been so overwhelming. His life, he realised, was losing its shape. All the colour and taste had been slowly drained and he felt helpless against the slow leak. He had gone to a gun store, and applied for a permit. Testing the guns woke up some hidden part of his body that was still vital. Perhaps it was blood-thirst, or morbid machismo. Whatever it had been, he didn't really understand it. All he felt was a sense of relief when he held the .357 and felt its power.

Thinking about the SIG, he remembered the night with one of his lovers. The purchase of the gun had given him brief respite from the asphyxiating emptiness he had felt. But it didn't last. He took a new lover from his pool of delicate neurotics. The danger of fucking his patients had long since died but in some vain attempt to rekindle that sensation of waking, their relationship had grown increasingly theatrical. Her masochistic tendencies amused him at first. He recalled how she had been vaguely dissatisfied when he hadn't successfully fucked the terror into her.

He was usually able to frighten his lovers with his monumental detachment which was an admittedly monstrous growth in his personality. He could see that his lack of care was an anomalous tumour of emptiness that seemed to grow and spread to every new lover. Yet on some nameless level he despised the women who let him behave this way. He despised them because the failed to wake anything in him beyond the Cartesian functions of the clock body. Even more paradoxically, since he selected his lovers from his clientele, the intrinsic nature of the doctor/patient relationship formed the roles in the bedroom fairly succinctly and decisively. He was always assigned the position of authority and power, and he found this responsibility wearying and boring.

On one such night, he had failed in his chore of drawing a scream out of her. They lay there on the bed in mute dissatisfaction and as if to relieve the lack of authentic tension, she had rolled onto her side and said listlessly. Have you ever seen a snuff film?

Myth. He responded not moving. Yet he was curious enough to fight drifting into sleep. Why do you ask? he said after a while. He continued to stare at the ceiling.

I think it would be really hot to watch one, don't you?

No.

Well, I want to find one. I want to fuck you while we're watching one. I've never seen anyone die. Have you?

Yes.

What's it like? She was getting warmer.

Not what you think.

Suddenly her presence angered him. He loathed her vulgar desires. Such a banal expression of sex mixed with death.

Tell me.

No. He still hadn't moved, but he did enjoy the rising feeling of hatred which was better than no feeling at all.

Do you think such films exist? I do. Humans are too perverse to stay away from it.

He turned his head and looked at her. Her presence was contaminating his room.

You want to star in one? I can arrange it. He smiled.

Fuck you, she said. You never listen to me. She was getting wet. He could smell it coming up from between her thighs, from her armpits. He could smell the arteries in her wrists swell.

He got up from the bed and went to the dresser and pulled the key from the chain around his neck. He unlocked the upper drawer and pulled out the .357. He turned around slowly and pointed it at her. Is this what you want? Is this what you mean?

She stared at him doe-eyed and pretty. She nearly came, her body sliding towards the first stage of a low-impact orgasm.

Jesus. I've never seen a real gun. Let me hold it. She rolled on her belly and reached for the SIG.

He stepped away from her, but continued pointing the gun at her. The safety was still on, but he planned to take it off in a matter of seconds. He had seen what gunshot wounds could do. His cock started getting harder.

This is turning you on, she said, smiling.

Lie down, he said.

No. I want to —

Lie down. His words had stopping power. She fell back against the sheet with a fleshy thud.

Close your eyes.

Oh, come on, Simon.

Do it.

She closed her eyes. He felt a sickening bile churn in his stomach. He took the ammo cartridge out of the gun and set it on the dresser.

What did you just do? she said. Her voice had a tremor of excited fear. He could practically see it growing inside her belly, pushing, bursting out towards her extremities.

I'm loading it.

He took a handkerchief from the drawer and went to the bed. Before he moved any closer to her body, he stopped. He knew that when he crossed the invisible line that was keeping him from touching her, he wouldn't be able to see her anymore. He didn't want to fuck her again. He didn't want to decipher her problems with her mother or her husband. He didn't care anymore. The decision took the time of synaptic flight. Enough to form the word. Yes.

He leaned over her and set the gun next to her head on the bed.

I can feel how close it is, she said hoarsely. It has a powerful energy to it.

It's going to get stronger.

She giggle-moaned. The slight inauthenticity of it tipped him all the way into the perverse game he had previously only been slightly tangled in. This particular round wouldn't last long, and then he would be alone again. Feeling the private pains of rage kept him alive by the merit of the fact that they were the only floats in the desolation of his interior life.

I'm going to cover your eyes, he said.

She didn't respond, and so he took her silence as an affirmation. He leaned over her and covered her eyes.

Maybe we shouldn't…I mean, you could make a mistake and —

Yes. I could make a mistake. Do you want me to stop? He drew away. His voice was so cold it froze the curtains and pillows. The sounds cracked and broke in the silence.

No, she said finally.

Don't make sudden movements. This gun is very sensitive.

Lying to her and blindfolding her had aroused him. He rubbed his cock against the full crescent of her outer breast.

She shuddered a little and when it looked as if she might create another pseudo-sex sound, he withdrew his cock and replaced it with the black Teflon nozzle of the gun. She stiffened but didn't say anything.

He dragged the gun across her nipples slowly and she arched her back slightly to meet the metal finger.

Don't move, he said sharply and she quickly flattened against the bed.

He brought the SIG to her neck and then dragged it up the soft flesh her under her chin. He waited there, and remembered seeing the remnants of failed suicides when he interned in an ER. Maya was right. With smaller fire arms the angle had to be just so. But with a gun like the .357. Close range. If he wanted to, he could remove her face from her skull with one easy, smooth squeeze. He stared at the meeting of the tip of metal against her jugular. He watched the way the gun aroused and started to frighten her was starting to wake the smouldering fire in his belly that was stoked when he originally bought the gun. He was pleased that she could not see his erection, or the effect her helplessness was having on him. It would have given her too much power.

He dragged the gun up her chin and then around to her temple. He waited there for a moment so that she could contemplate the career of a bullet through the soft tissue of her brain, barely concealed under the fragile bone of skull and hair. He brought the tip of the barrel to her lip.

Suck it, he said.

She opened her mouth and took the gun against her lips. He pushed further and she let it slip deeper into her throat. He almost laughed at the absurdity of the scenario, the cliché of cock and gun. But simultaneously he was engaged in the moment, and it felt dangerously diseased. It was this night that he realised that he had lost any authentic will towards health.

She sucked his SIG like a whore on cock. He withdrew it from her mouth and she gasped a little but said nothing. The electricity had been conducted from her tongue through the grip of the gun like a seal. He went to the dresser and put the 10 round cartridge back into the gun.

What are you doing?

Checking the ammo, he replied.

He went back to her body and dragged the gun past the soft cup of her neck, down the boney plate of her sternum and then over the softer ridge of her abdomen. When he got closer to her pudenda, her body rebelled slightly. He watched the muscle tension come and go in her jaw. He liked watching her struggle; a butterfly against his pin.

Don't hurt me, she said weakly.

Don't move too suddenly, he said quietly, now meaning it. The fact that he had a loaded gun near her cunt made him want to laugh maniacally, dizzily with the absurdity of the moment. He was after all a psychiatrist. But his passion for science and symbol had splintered was becoming a deformed psychic golem over which he had no control. He concentrated on sliding the nose of the gun towards her clit. It was like a bullet sitting just beyond it's gun, glistening like a small metal ball between the full vulvular envelope. He drew the edge of the nozzle towards her clit and then slightly caressed it. Without warning, he started to ease the nozzle inside her. Her breath shot up from her lower belly. He watched the tendons in her hands lift and strain against the fragile skin of her debutante hands.

Simon — she breathed.

Shut up, he said, very quietly. Shut up, or I'll shoot you. I swear to fucking God, I will. The words passed from his lips before he was sure of their truth. He wasn't sure any more what a truth would look or feel like.

Please, she said. I think we —

Shut up.

The gun was sliding further into her and with every centimetre of metal insertion, the room swelled with a sweating surreality. He felt a tear of perspiration run down his left cheek. Her breathing was growing hot and shallow and it was changing the climate in the room. Her breath was changing the shape of the bedroom and her body and his body. Her pussy was melting the gun. It bled up into her and she pushed against the meltdown.

He slid a finger inside her, and rested it next to the barrel of the gun. His finger merged with the gun and her cunt. The fear of himself, of her, and of the place he was taking them was a fire that was burning away all definitions and separations. He pushed the gun in deeper and put his other hand around the shaft of his penis. The harder he pumped the gun into her, the more he was able to clearly imagine the anatomical implications of a bullet path blazing through her interior. She was nearing orgasm, but maintained a bodily stillness that betrayed her obedience. He stopped jacking off just before he came. His muscles seized up and cramp spread to various sectors of his body.

I want you to come, he said. Now.

And she did. Quietly and without a lot of useless motion. Her cunt lips squeezed around the black Teflon and the gun cooked inside her.

I wish you could see how this looks to me, he said, without emotion.

She was wasted inside her terror. She was listening to the metal against the sides of her tight flesh gaps and then she couldn't hear anything except for the overexposed internal screech of the orgasm. Her breathing halted. The room shattered and broke.

When he guided her to the door, he noticed that his hands were shaking when he locked the dead bolt. He told her not to come back again. He felt that if he kept fucking her it was going to lead to something permanent — such as death.

He had never seen her again.

A successful psychiatrist, Lazar knew how to utilise the simple and powerful mechanism of repression. And he used this common tool to blot out the memory of the gun episode; but Maya's book had dragged the memory out. He found that it had not aged well over time. It was uglier than he remembered, and worse, it still aroused him. It made him mildly sick to think that had taken such a risk with an unlocked handgun. Fucking his patients was an enormous professional and personal gamble. Yet the potential catastrophe that he unconsciously sought eluded him, and so he kept doing it.

XVI

Switch

"Simon, what the hell is going on?" Anna's voice was transparent with fear. It was glass and it came through the holes of the phone and cut his lip.

"What do you mean?"

"I called your office. What's going on? What the hell is going on in this shitty world." She spat the words. The warmth had been siphoned from her.

"Are you all right?"

"Yes," he replied, as calm as a murderer. A liar. A thief.

"Can't you tell me what's going on? Simon, I need you right now. I really need…" She stopped, almost choking on the words.

"I needed some time off," he replied. "I'm tired." He watched himself talking on the phone to his best friend. He felt nothing, and he knew that the break from his former self was truly authentic. His nausea and malaise had always been relieved by Anna. Now he simply wanted to avoid the responsibility of being kind. He waited for her to speak.

"She has marks on her," Anna said. "She came home with marks all over her body." The emotion in her voice started to drain away.

St. John. A nerve pinched in his cortex. He sat up straight.

"Oh, Simon. . . I"

"What kind of marks?" He tried to swallow the queer vibrato that started in his throat.

"Oh, Christ, Simon, I don't know what the fuck he did to her. But she's a mess."

"Slow down. Tell me what happened."

"I don't know. She won't tell me."

"When did she get home?" His curiosity was driving him back into his body.

"Around 6 am," Anna's voice was still dull.

"What did she say when she came home? Where did she say she had been?"

"With St. John. That was it. I got really pissed and demanded an explanation, and she just looked at me. Her eyes, Simon," Anna paused. He could hear her trying to get a professional grip on the personal mayhem. "Her eyes were glassy. Dead. It was really creepy. So not like Jade. I don't understand at all. I mean I know she's flirted with SM stuff before, but it has never been a feature of our relationship because you know how I feel about that and — "

"How do you feel about it?"

"It's regressed. It's destructive. It's infantile and violent and I won't participate in the degradation of another human."

"Maybe she wanted that."

"I don't know. I don't see how anyone would want to be tortured."

He smiled soundlessly.

"Did she fuck him?"

"I don't know. She wouldn't talk. She wouldn't let me touch her. I tried to get a look at the welts and punctures...she had cigarette burns on her breasts and legs but she wouldn't let me get near her. Even as a physician."

"So what did you do?"

"I left her alone. She was sleeping when I left. I'm at my office and I don't know what to do."

"I think you should just let her work it out and then come to you with her explanation. Pushing her is probably going to drive it underground. And then it will become a powerful secret. That is when it gets dangerous."

"It already is, Simon. It already is."

Lazar handed out some bland panaceas to Anna and then rang off. He was more eager to examine his feelings about the conversation than he was in actually continuing it. He was surprised at himself, wondering how this lack of affect had drifted into his relationship with Anna. It had happened so quickly. The obvious link was meeting St. John, but he could not rest it entirely upon a stranger who had upset him. St. John, he decided was a symbol and it was this symbol that cleaved him from Anna and any illusory world of balance and harmony. But what St. John and Maya represented continued to elude any kind of clear revelation.

It seemed that St. John intended to wreck the domestic quiet of Jade's life. The way it seemed from where Lazar stood was that Jade's hunger to launch a new project with a powerful agent made her weak. Easy prey. And St. John was clarifying that humiliating desire for success by literally debasing her. Lazar admired the mercenary work of St. John. It was the way that Maya fucked her suicides. He thought he might be getting a clearer idea of Maya's *modus operandi* while St. John's remained perplexing. Perhaps, Lazar thought, the man was simply cruel. He was surprised that apparent sadism had crept into St. John's professional life. Lazar smiled ironically at the thought that St. John had behaved unprofessionally. But what did professionalism really mean anymore?

He got lost in a maze of mysterious half-formed images when he thought of St. John hurting Jade. Sado-masochism didn't really seem to fit into the persona that St. John had presented at Anna's dinner party. It always amazed Lazar at the creativity of the human mind in its quest to sew together the fragments of other personalities in desperate attempts at personal cohesion. Lazar was pleased that St. John was not coming together easily. When he considered the pictures of St. John dominating Jade they seemed vaguely impossible, almost comical. The accessories and accoutrements of SM play seemed excessive and almost ridiculous when he considered St. John.

St. John's profound lack of a carnal scent bothered Lazar's memory. Perhaps he hadn't been the one that had marked Jade. That would explain St. John's question at the dinner party.

Are you a voyeur?

Lazar distinctly recalled St. John's fastidious appearance and what seemed to be a subtle embarrassment about the occupancy in something so unpredictable and vulgar as a body. He couldn't imagine St. John to be the sort to suggest a whipping or a pair of handcuffs.

Somewhere within, Lazar found that he was pleased that he had professionally read St. John correctly. There certainly were deeply hidden perversions that called out for an unveiling. Why else had he left the card in his pocket?

When he looked at it from that perspective, a fresh energy coursed through his body. He would use Anna's pain as an excuse to call St. John. He would call St. John as a professional. He laughed out loud at the irony.

He picked up Maya's journal and flipped to the crease that held St. John's stained business card. He slipped the card in his breast pocket. He decided he would call on Anna's behalf. Lazar had a moment's hesitation when he realised that his motivations were dubious and self-serving; he paused and observed himself. What did it matter any more what his motives were? He wanted to get closer to understanding St. John. That was enough.

He felt he had two patients now to look after and they were more than enough.

It was only early afternoon, and Lazar wrestled with the idea of calling St. John. He battled the hesitation, yet enjoyed the anxiousness that waiting was producing in him. He held off calling until he felt humiliated by his schoolgirl skittishness.

A cool British receptionist answered. When she asked Lazar the nature of his business, he faltered.

"I am returning Mr St. John's call," he said finally.

He was put on hold for a long while, and then the receptionist came back on the line and told him that St. John was in a meeting and would phone back later.

Lazar hung up the phone feeling thwarted and angry. While he was waiting on the line he had successfully convinced himself that he had sincerely called on behalf of his friends. On behalf of the inadvertent plea for help that St. John had left by way of his calling card. The fragile delusion was shattered when St. John refused to receive him.

He wanted to get out of the apartment. Suddenly, he wondered if he hadn't made an enormous mistake in taking leave of his patients and his practice. Yet when he thought about it, his practice had long ceased to be an anchor in his life. When he thought of it practically, he didn't really know what other options he had than to take a break. He had already hurt so many of them. He found that he didn't feel badly about it. When he thought about all the patients he had fucked, all the patients he had ignored or subtly belittled, he searched his body, his mind, his memory for some feeling of regret. Nothing.

He put on his coat to leave, but the threat of missing the phone call drove him back inside. He poured a drink. It was early, and he had nowhere to go but back to Maya. He brought the bottle with him.

XVII
Lady Orgasma

*t*he hotel room has shrunk. I have plundered the Servi-Bar and there is no more candy. No more million dollar nuts. No more crackers. Tiny booze bottles klink, empty. I'm out of cigarettes. I can't bear to use that ridiculous instrument of torture, the phone. The maids knock on the door and I send them away. The phone rang until I pulled the cord. What's left? My clothes hate me. They mock me from their casual positions on the chairs and floor. The mirrors have been properly dealt with.

Like a ragged Alice, Maya 29 has plunged one foot through the glass, but she missed the artery. Botched suicides are infinitely more tragic than their success. I am destined to stay until it is done.

Dopey from the violence, Maya 11 stumbled and fell. She let Maya 12 slip through her weak fingered lust, opening the cavity and changing souls like socks. Maya 12 half-baked and still searching, suicided in an economy car. Japanese make. It was cramped and without style. No V8 engine. No roar. Little zip, and a thanks for the ride, baby. She left behind a wrong phone number and directions to someone else's house.

I don't need to see or remember them. They were cheap vehicles. Like my mind which is filled with tawdry entertainments and tacky diversions, a lot of suicides are disposable. So Maya 13 slipped into Planet Disease expecting nothing but a mediocre and plotless movie and a febrile nap. The usual fuckless death. But thirteen is a lucky number in a trick world.

Reminder: Don't mix love and suicide. It's such a mess to clean up. The stains won't come out of the grout. You end up carrying them around.

Maya 13. Longest shelf-life to date.

He out-suicided me in the end and so, in some way, Maya 13 was never properly memorialised.

At first, I thought he was just a brand new suicide in a purple package. His bright blue eye caught me in its glance across a crowded old cafeteria in Pasadena. There was a lot of talk in the room. Too much talk and smoke and mindless prattle about the unimportance of art. Indifference to hope. Fashionable despair. His blue eye caught me with its sharp pin, and without pomp, destroyed a little bit of my ignorance in its gaze. It was as though he tore off my jewellery so there was less distraction. Less noise. It was not love, something more elemental. Wordless.

From the other side of his head, his brown eye said: Sex. He simply got up, crossed over all the shit. He walked over the backs of all the other suicides and said: Come home with me now. Come home. I want to make love to you.

Wily with confusion, Maya 13 darted back into the crowd and pulled the smoke around her head. Something about him did not jive. He did not have the suicide barking from his body.

I wanted to smell him. She wanted to leave. Cross-purpose entered the body, strafing the rib cage, the pelvis. The cunt.

His face, his wandering eye, and his purple shirt indicated the new but not the novel. He was old, but had a young man's body and drive. It's simple, his eye indicated. Let's go home and fuck. Let's see what the body yields.

You'll get more than you bargain for, I said. Thinking of the wound. Always thinking of the wound.

He smiled easily. He didn't need Maya 13. He shrugged 'OK' and turned to go.

I was suspicious of tricks, suspicious of a botched suicide, but I followed him cautiously behind. He took us home.

Purple is the colour of orgasm.

He showed me a new and improved method of suicide. Death through the portal of pleasure. She stood in front him waiting for the blow, leaning forward for the punch. He unbuttoned her shirt slowly. His hands were brown and had scratches and nicks all over them from hard work. He rested his palm on her stomach for a moment, not looking at her face, but at her body. He moved his rough fingers up her sternum and showed her what her breasts were for. He drew the connection between nipple and cunt easily. He dropped a plumb line of raw sensation down the middle of her.

Can't you see the wound, she said, startled. Indignant. He wasn't reacting to the mess. The sutures and resutures. The seeping.

Yes, he said. I see it. He didn't stop in his investigation of her shape and form.

She waited impatiently before him. Some had lied and told her the scars were beautiful, just to get inside; but once their hands were in, they always changed their minds. Others would admit the wound was disgusting, thus they had privilege to get inside because it wasn't anything but a trash can to throw the occasional letter in. Some books. A few photographs.

He didn't say anything except: Are you going to help me get these boots off?

Still looking for the violence catch, she leaned over and pulled at the worn boot. It smelled of Wyoming. His hair smelled like a tree. She stood there stupid with the boot. This moment was unrecognisable. Unfamiliar and soothing. His hands were large and square and he pulled her down on to the floor. She noticed his body for the first time. He stretched out beside her like an alien object. Open to her scrutiny, he calmly waited. She knelt beside him and ran her hands over his smooth torso. Her hands got caught up in the velocity of his form and slid quickly down his rib cage and towards the meeting point of pelvis and abdomen, the pronounced male slope of hip and stomach. The previous suicides flashed in her mind. They seemed clothed and sanitary. Without nudity. She wondered how she had managed to have so much sex and never see a body before. He reached up and put his hand on the back of her neck and the curl of his fingers gave substance to that part of her body. She leaned into the tug of desire. Fear was stripped away. She smiled, knowing it was grotesque. He didn't notice. He kissed her and his saliva was warm and sweet with the residue of Copenhagen.

His motions had a clarity that was not inspired by drug or rage and she was uncertain in her interpretation of it. He didn't speak, instead moving with a slow certainty that was a language in its own right. He had carpenter's hands that knew how to disrobe the moment with efficiency and care. They lay on the wood floor naked together. Maya 13 instinctively reached down and covered her pussy, never having been seen naked before.

Let me see that. He laughed a little and pulled her hands away replacing them with his own. He wasn't mocking her.

Just laughing. He put one hand on the curve of her waist while the other worked at the soft wet skin of her cunt. She felt smaller near him but not reduced by his size or confidence. He didn't need to employ the usual methods of suicide to get what he wanted from her. The usual throb of the wound was distant. She panicked. This was going to be a useless exercise if there wasn't going to be a murder. Maya 13 prepared to add him to a growing list of forgettable suicides. She opened her legs and readied to spear her body over his.

Wait, he said evenly. I want to make you come first. I want to watch you.

She didn't know what he meant.

Let me, he said.

He slid his hands between her thighs and separated them. He licked his fingers and then easily slipped into her pussy. He put his other hand over the wound, discreetly holding the edges of it together. She looked into his seeing eye and then the blind one and realised that he had a bunch of suicide in him. There was a wound somewhere on his body that she couldn't see. Comprehension spread through her body, more startling and piercing than pain. She grabbed his neck and pulled his warm head closer. She tasted his mouth and there was the hint of blood and sadness there. Maya 13 was the first Maya that shoved the dormant manifestation back inside the womb. Do not move, she told Maya 14. Stay asleep for awhile. Do not wake. Let me stay.

No kick inside.

Let me, he said and raised her body up from the ground.

He was my only humanity suicide. He is the lasting sadness.

He gave me a Purple Heart tattoo just below the wound. Pulling me up over his body he showed me the secret map to planets of orgasm. He described with his fingers the round globe of the clit and the motions of his hips fused to mine created a universe of movement. Music of bones moving the constellations of cells and skin. He showed me how to hold the wound closed. He gave me a prolonged life and then he died, my legs straddling around him, my arms around his neck, clinging there. I had no bardo to tell him. No gift to give him except the memory of pleasure that he wrote on the inside of my body.

Don't leave me, Maya 13 cried as her body crested on the first orgasm. Her breasts shot forward, the intensity of their bodies unified. Gemini lovers humping and clawing at the tail end of this life's pleasure.

I'm not going anywhere, he said. Come on to bed, he would say. And she stayed awhile. Holding the edges of the wound shut so we wouldn't be dragged in just yet. But the drive towards suicide ended up swallowing the courage to stop. Maya 14 started to wake.

The fierce grief of inevitable loss blended with the passion and Maya 13 finally tore at the edges of the wound in the blindness of the final orgasm. She shot through a ceiling of plate glass and the fictional cosmology that they built with their hands, their feet, their lips and words shattered and fell around the bed. Maya 13 at last uncovered the wound and reaching in, yanked Maya 14 out by the neck and threw her back to Planet Disease. Maya 14 stood over their bed, and Maya 13 found the hole and climbed inside.

I have to leave, I said.

Don't go. Come on up to bed, he said.

I can't be with you anymore. I was in the middle of a frustrated suicide just out of his sight. I didn't want to hurt him. I have to leave, I said again, struggling to kill it. Maya 14 was waking. Yawning. Stretching.

This is the special eulogy to him because he changed the

shape and hue of all the remaining suicides. He crowned me with the wordless fixture of love and contaminated the purity of hatred that had been heretofore working the machinations of the wound. But, the wound cannot be healed; not even by his memory. But the suicides did change shape after he died.

When I commit him to the pages, the wound ceases to hurt and becomes the self entire. I am closer to her than ever. I am almost her.

XVIII

Stay Sweet —
Eulogy Number 14

What? I misunderstood what he said into the phone on the other side.

I have it, he said.

Have what?

It. I've got it. The virus. Death. I'm holding it in the palm of my hand. Pieces of paper that say yes. Yes, you have it.

It's not a death sentence, I heard myself say.

He laughed and then choked on the emptiness.

Fear took root when he said the words, and it grew while we talked. For a moment, I lost the edges of the body. It was nothing more than a clay figure sitting on the edge of the small wooden chair in the kitchen. But the centrifugal force of his voice brought me back. Back home, inside the endangered body teetering on the edge of the world. I held the phone tighter, as if clutching it more firmly would gain purchase on an imploding world.

He said, I'm Positive.

The words lay on the kitchen floor like the dead mouse I'd found earlier in the day. Nowhere to put it. A feeling in the body flowered around the wound. His words were directly linking sex, death, the wound. It was no longer some kind of poetic conceit, no longer some kind of abstraction. With incredible speed, it grew into a tree with venomous branches strangling every corner of the room. A red tree, with the poison fruit.

I AM POSITIVE.

The night radiated hot air that deprived the world of oxygen. I said nothing.

He kept talking, breathless intonations that hinted at the inevitable grief. His voice interrogated the language, disbelief and realisation competing for dominance. I pictured his mouth carefully framing every syllable.

I wanted you to know because... his teeth cut into the cadence.

When real death entered the kitchen all ambiguity was destroyed except for the sound of his weeping. It was so similar to the sound of his laughter that everything was confused for a moment. Then the clarity started to raze the house, delineating everything seen and unseen. A split-ended nerve shot through the middle of the wound.

What about me? I thought.

I sicken now at the self-reflection. I could shatter like a bad luck mirror. I could be. I might be.

POSITIVE.

I held on to the phone, my only remaining umbilicus to him. He delivered more news, mouth to mouth. Just as we used to kiss. Directly. Simply without the theatrics of false eroticism. I waited, quiet.

What could a body say in this accidental world? Nothing.

I considered comforting him, but the words curled up and dried on the tongue.

Instead, her left hand went to my body as if to soothe it, while the right hand kept fear at bay, fingers delicately clipping the wound shut like a robe.

I will die, he said.

Yes, Maya 20 said.

It had been some time since we talked. Some suicides had come between us. But we were back at death again. Forever joined. Gemini twins.

This is what fear really looks like I thought. We were inside it together as we were when we made love. We were inside the whale.

We were once so...I couldn't finish the sentence. I looked down at my hands, at my breasts and regarded the Maya 20 body with great wonder.

This has been the constant vehicle of our demise. Yet it is such a complicated vessel, curlicued with pleasure and laughter and memory. The body will inevitably be a tree bearing the apple.

There must be a mistake, I said, lamely.

To herself she thought, I have died so many times since. I'm supposed to die before you. That was our unspoken contract.

Don't leave me, I said, an echo of the past. His hair smelled like trees. She remembered the memory of the 13th and how he had quietly held her wound shut for her as long as he could.

I looked down the front of her chest. The body became more remote. It was spontaneously dangerous and unfamiliar.

The blood was revolting. I could hide in the cunning of language for a while longer, but soon the facts would became as certain as the unutterable and true name of God.

I felt the colour drain from my face, and watched the metamorphosis in the mirror as I held the phone. It became a strange series of shapes and angles unrecognisable as myself but sharply defined as parts. The wooden body. A pearl of sweat fell from one of her nipples.

My skin is weeping. She found herself afraid of her own body, all the forgotten parts around the wound had become unknown. I had focused so much on the wound. A series of empty chambers rolling over, the heart is a bewildered roulette. There is no good description for the certain ruin of a body. His body. Inaudible screams from galaxies yet to be born suddenly came out from the constellation of the pelvis.

I'll never have children, he said finally.

Their earth lurched and stopped. She said nothing. He will no longer be. To be. The identity of the self with the body. Forever wedded.

The shape of this unknown region is beyond my weak power of description. I'm out of cigarettes. Dead 29 times over and still don't understand this moment between us. I am humiliated by my lack of insight and disgusted by my cowardice. The instinctive voice was as insistent as the body itself.

What about me?

The final cry of all suicides. Echo and Narcissus.

We held each other though the phone and time moved in a curious, lacerated montage of overlapping images that crossbred and bled. Lovers and bruises. Sloppy sad drunk nights. His pepperminted and sawdust smell and the curl of the lamplight on his shoulder and lip, burnt umber night sun from Alameda and Sixth coming in and the fruit trucks waking us and him saying from above in the loft, *Are you going to come on up? Come on up here.*

Raggedy home, sweet and dirty. The kissing wall.

No, I said. I can't be with you anymore. Turning away. Deals and requests to uncertain deities were suddenly forgivable.

I understand their fictions now. Truth and fear are now one. Forever hold your peace.

Cautiously, I dragged my eyes around the kitchen. False moves or clumsy gestures could have shattered the suddenly precious body. I stood very still while the checkerboard tiles of the kitchen floor slid crazily. I remember that outside the barred window, summer insisted and pulsed. Lush life. The redundant sense of terror lulled me. The sunflowers from the hardware store just planted continued to push against the soil, continue to push through each catastrophe. Green arteries of nature pulsed in spite of the city's disregard. Wildflowers shyly bloomed.

The Argus-eyed cat draped around a blue bowl on the scarred kitchen table was a miracle, as was the garden, a sudden green jewel in the sewage of New York.

Is it my time? Is it growing in me now? The difference between suicide and murder became clear. Willful suicides seemed suddenly stupid. I said nothing and held the wound shut. Wanting to disappear from shame.

I held on to the phone so we wouldn't slip off the side of the earth while thermodynamic events occurred in small nine-stitched increments.

I think you better go to Wyoming, to that big university. Get checked over there. I think they made a mistake...

Her hand reached out to an article on the table. Her fingers moved over the words. "Why I Photograph Clouds," by Arthur Stieglitz. The fear was drifting. It had to be a mis —

I did go to Wyoming. To the university.

He wanted to make good paintings. I was already thinking of him in the past tense. Amazing, the finesse of deconstructing a corpse in memory before a body is dead. He wanted to be a good person. He made things, gave birth to wood things with his hands.

Fear infected the universe.

I don't need this, he said.

The summer insisted. Breathed. The seeds were going to turn their tricks and the sapling grew monstrous up from my kitchen floor like a red Siamese candelabrum.

I don't want to die, he said.

But he did, and before he went, he said: Stay sweet, and I thought, what a strange thing to say.

XIX

Thermodynamics

Lazar started to cry. No sound came out of his throat. No constriction in the chest or face. The tears just came out of his eyes easily. They spilled over his cheeks spontaneously and without satisfaction. The phone was ringing. He let it go. The book slipped to his knees and he looked down at his feet trapped in the expensive shoes. One foot was turned at an odd angle and the shape of his helplessness was encapsulated in the gesture. The sound that was caught in his throat finally squeezed out in a long anguished O. He was so tired.

The grief and loss that he had managed to elude caught him by surprise. It broadsided him and laid him out. His mind flooded with memories. Fragments of his patients' pain were intertwined with his own. He thought of his failed marriage. Maya's grief and torment braided with his own sense of emptiness.

He realised that up until this moment, he had been reading

her words as fiction, and he was understanding her as an alluring abstraction. That is what had made her so appealing to him. But suddenly something more tangible tore through his will to see the words as fictions. He had not regarded Maya as a person, but rather as an object of superficial scrutiny. He realised that he had not even wondered until now where she was on a day to day basis. How she survived. If she had friends. Family. It seemed so unlikely. He realised that he had just thought of her as safe in his drawer next to the gun, animated only by his interaction with her. Now, he wondered if she was alive or dead. If she was indeed in a hotel somewhere waiting for the courage to visit. The fortitude to kill herself.

Yet despite his lack of humanistic curiosity about her, he identified with her struggle in some way that had never connected him to another woman in quite the same way. He was filled with a grotesque kind of longing to follow Maya into her wound. He was stunned by the sudden need to find her. He laughed hollowly through the tears: he had fallen in love for the first time in his life.

He thought of Catherine and his chest tightened and then caved. Reading about Maya's experience of falling in love reminded him of a time when he thought he loved Catherine. He was so far from that now, and when he regarded the pathos of his foot — a twisted and inadvertent attachment to his leg — he felt that it was just as the rest of his body; an accidental attachment to his soul. He wondered how he had arrived at the place where he was.

He regarded the narrative line of his life. He had, until recently, thought of his profession as a prophylactic against the fear of death. He had soothed patients from their fear of love. He had spent his time vivisecting these fundamental elements of life only to realise as he sat in his expensive apartment alone, that they were immutable — that all his educated dissections were pointless and had left him alone and numb. Maya was waking him and the sudden surprise of feeling was uncomfortable and entirely compelling.

When his marriage to Catherine started to fail, he was able to take it apart under his psychic scalpel. Carefully he looked at each part and pointed out the flaws, both his and hers. He watched the protracted death of their relationship as he stood far away from his body and hers. He absorbed the loss in a muffled way that had been shocking to Catherine. They had been apart for over a year and he still couldn't bear the stricken look on her face when they met. She watched him as though he was a stranger and indeed he had become alienated from her, from everyone.

When she found out about his infidelities she didn't cry and he remembered that he had been a little disappointed. He realised now that he had wanted to watch her cry. But her lasting disappointment and sadness was the final pall that was slowly dragged over their relationship. Finally she wandered away like a whipped dog and he hated her for it. It was the closest he could get to feeling anything for her. A woman he had been married to for ten years.

The lack of sensation he felt towards Catherine and the disintegration of their relationship was similar to the detachment he felt about his patients' pain. Nothing was penetrating him. Nothing until Maya's book got a hold of him. He couldn't even exactly explain its effect, or the fact that he began to feel that he was effecting a certain kind of change upon the book. He laughed at his own pathetic hope that he was, in some metaphysical and invisible way, having an effect on Maya's life by reading it.

Lazar sat crying, realising that something within him had just stopped. It had been some years ago when he gave in to the inertia. It was abrupt and so shocking, he could not bring himself to do anything about this emotional stasis because in doing something about it he would be recognising the problem. So he did nothing when the stasis occurred and soon his psyche began to atrophy. His marriage died and for a while his practice had been the one handle that he gripped, while the rest of his life slipped off the side of his stilled internal planet.

Finally he began having affairs with his patients in half-hearted attempts to jump-start some kind of feeling. Indeed, feelings were stirred in him but their source was all from the same despairing place. The existential virus was consuming him.

Anna had been a gentle inoculate against the virus. But then she knew nothing of his affairs with his patients. He had kept it from her because it would have easily destroyed their friendship. She was an ethical physician. She would have probably even turned him into the AMA, so in effect Lazar's relationship with Anna was superficial and a lie. Even so, her calm disposition had been a source of relief to Lazar in the past few years. But the recent appearance of St. John had upset that somehow. His mind turned again to Maya and he found himself objectively interested in the fact that he consistently linked St. John and Maya.

Still tears poured effortlessly down his face. When he thought of Maya as a breathing woman, he recalled the intense attraction he had felt for her when she came to his office. Her visit seemed so long ago, he could only vaguely remember what she looked like, but he could certainly remember her smell. He thought that she was likely alone. He had watched enough mentally ill people alienate everyone around themselves. He did know that there had been something fundamentally askew about her when she had come to him. He feared that she was no longer was alive and this made him cry harder. It had been too long since he had this kind of release. Suddenly the urge to find her, to help her, to fuck her, overwhelmed him.

It was interesting to him that the mention in her journal of a death outside herself had made him think of her in terms of the living. He told himself he could love her and that it would help her. Even the absurdity of his thoughts did not thwart the feeling. He stood and realised that he had no recourse to her except through the book. Perhaps, if he flipped to the end he would find the necessary clues but something kept him from doing it. As if he were to do it, he would somehow kill her. He felt confused and maddened. Exhausted. The tears were stopping, and the phone started ringing again.

He stood unmoving for a moment in the centre of his apartment. He felt the irrational sensation that the next voice he heard would crack his grief and loss in two, either pushing him back to where he had been; a state of numbed indifference, or it would force him forward into the dark world of undifferentiated chaos. He was amazed at the fragility of the moment. He felt that he was standing on the cusp of something great that was cloaked inside an inconsequential instant. The telephone continued to ring. Chaos theory. Flapping of a butterfly in flight. Molecular shifts. The wheel turned. He let the book slip to the floor and felt relief, as though by severing the contact with the journal, the feelings were already starting to recede. He answered the telephone.

"Dr Lazar?"

"Yes." He stopped weeping instantly. The feelings were strangled in his throat.

"It's William St. John." There was a long pause.

"Yes. Mr St. John. Hello. I'm glad you phoned."

"Call me William," St. John said.

Lazar lurched forward into the unknown.

They arranged to meet for dinner later that night. The plans were laid very succinctly and without much frill. Even though there was no outward expression of emotion, Lazar sensed a crackling tension between them. He was not sure of its nexus, nor did he want to analyse it. The weeping had stopped and Lazar already felt slightly ridiculous for the display. He regarded the book accusingly on the floor between the coffee table and the couch. He didn't want to touch it, feeling superstitious enough to think that if he made contact with it, the sadness would flood him again. He left it where it was, awkward and bent on the floor. The brief exchange with St. John had cauterised the feelings of loss for the moment. As he moved around his apartment, he found that he was strangely excited. He intuited some change coming but he wasn't sure what it was. He sat down and phoned Anna.

"Anna, this is Simon."

"Oh, Simon." He waited but she didn't say any more.

"I spoke to St. John."

"You did? Why?"

"I want to help you get to the bottom of this, Anna. I don't want to see you or Jade get hurt. Especially by someone like him." Lazar's eyes wandered back to Maya's book as he held the receiver. He walked over and lightly kicked it with his toe under the couch. Even then, a little electricity shot through his body. The corner of the book stuck out from under the couch, as if it were insisting on not going away. He left it.

"Oh, Simon," she said again. "I don't know. Maybe we should just leave it alone. I'm really confused about this. I'm so tired. I don't know what the right thing is anymore."

"Why don't you cancel your appointments for the day and go home?"

"I already did."

"Why aren't you home?"

She hesitated. "I don't want to be around Jade. When I

think of looking at her, I feel nauseous. I feel as though there's a stranger in the house and I can't go back there."

"What are you going to do."

"Get drunk," she said dully.

"What can I do?"

"Be careful," she said and then hung up.

The deviousness and the sincere urge to help his friend were confused. Finally he realised that he didn't know exactly why he was going to meet St. John for dinner but that he had to do it for himself first. Anything that followed would be incidental. The urgency about seeing St. John had displaced his need to see Maya, and he recognised this slip. He didn't care, so long as he didn't have to feel that grief again. He poured a drink and went to shower.

XX

Prosthetic Desire

Sado-masochism was no longer included in the DSMV. DSMV V — the standard diagnostic manual and psychiatrist's bible. The essential guide to all quantifiable disturbances of the mind. Until recently SM had been included as a perversion that should be recognised as a symptom by professionals. A disease that could be treated. As if one could be healed from such an illness. Anna laughed and ordered another drink.

Physician, heal thyself, she muttered drunkenly to herself. The man next to her said, *What?*

Nothing, she said. Can I bum a cigarette off you? And the man obliged. Menthol. Disgusting. She lit it and enjoyed the foulness of it. She deserved it.

Jade brought SM to the bedroom, and Anna had been unable to say no.

At first every fibre of her professional being rebelled. She could see the diagnosis on the page of the DSMV. At least when she thought about it in hindsight, she wished to remember herself as a reluctant sadist. But that was a delusion. She could see it all clearly now.

It started with the pictures. She and Jade were looking at a cheesy porn rag at a newsstand one night. Anna can't even remember why they had decided to look at the magazine in the first place, but they were and suddenly the page flipped open to a spread. A woman tied up to a bed. A woman with leg spreaders kneeling before another woman. Her face forced into the other's thighs. Anna flipped quickly past it, but Jade had stopped her. She reached over Anna's shoulder and went back to the pages of the woman tied to the bed spread-eagled, a blindfold and gag in her mouth. She put her finger on that image, and then dragged her hand down the glossy surface. Anna thought that it looked as if the pictures were covered with saliva. Jade's finger rested on the woman kneeling before the mistress.

Jade leaned forward and pushed her hips into Anna's ass and whispered in her ear, "I want you to do that to me, baby. Will you do that for me sometime? Will you tie me up and fuck me? I want you to take your cock and shove it up my ass."

Anna had been shocked. Not by what Jade was saying exactly, but at the pure bolt of excitement that ran through her centre. They had always had a good sexual relationship but it had never really turned kinky. It was a sudden revelation about Jade. About herself. Anna tried to stop the feeling from taking root inside. She did this by feigning an attitude of disinterest. She looked down at the shining image of the woman on the bed. Spread legs. Shaved pussy. Breasts pulled taut across the rib cage. Leather. Blindfolds. The woman kneeling. She wanted to think it was authentically ill and regressed, but she didn't.

"It turns you on, doesn't it, baby?" hissed Jade. "I want you to do it to me. Do me like that. I want you to hurt me. I want you to top me."

Anna snapped the magazine shut and turned around. She looked at Jade and said, "I don't ever want to hurt you."

But the seed had been planted.

"I want to know that you've fucked me. I want to know that I belong only to you." Jade whispered at Anna over the table at dinner that night.

"You don't already feel that way?"

Jade ignored the question. "I want to see the marks all over my body. Your marks. I want to be walking down the street feeling as though I'm owned by you. That you've pissed on me."

"God, that's the thing about porn, Jade. It just feeds the imagination with these vacuous images selling exploitation as pleasure. It's all wrong."

"I think they're honest," Jade said. "Those images and SM games just bring to the surface what is fundamentally true in our society. In human nature. It's all about power exchanges and exploitation."

"You've been reading Marx again," Anna tried to diffuse it.

"Besides that," Jade continued, "those pictures turned you on. I could tell. We've been together for almost eight months. Don't think that I can't tell what makes you hot."

"Jade, you know how I feel about this."

"No, I don't know how do you feel. Tell me. Talk to me. I want to know. I think you're just afraid. And brainwashed."

"Brainwashed? By what?"

"By your books. By the fucking DSMV. By your own profession," Jade said the last a little hesitantly.

"You don't know what you're talking about," Anna said. She was pushing her rage down. The heat was rising in visible waves from the table.

Anna furtively glanced around the restaurant.

"I'm not ashamed," Jade said, following her stare.

"I don't agree with you. I think that those kinds of power exchanges are unhealthy."

"Yes they are. But they are transformative. They bring to the surface what is hidden," Jade insisted. "And I thought that was your mission in life. To reveal secrets. To strip them bare. Well here's your chance for the real deal."

"Oh come on, what makes you think that sadomasochism is the real deal, Jade? Don't be ridiculous."

"And sitting in some office paying you a hundred and twenty-five dollars an hour to *talk* to *you* is the real thing?"

Couples on either side of their table were eating in silence, clearly embarrassed by the conversation they couldn't avoid. Jade focused on Anna with a fierce intensity.

"It's a hundred and twenty," said Anna trying to break the spell. Jade would not sway.

"I don't want to hurt you. Purposefully or otherwise." Anna said finally.

"I think you do."

"No. I don't."

"I'm going to find a way there. With or without you." Jade was starting to close down. "Anna…" she reached across the table. Anna drew her hand away.

"I don't understand where this is coming from, Jade. It's obviously not just the fucking magazine."

"It's important to me now. If you have to apply the tricks of your trade, then you will. But I'm not interested in analysing it in any other fashion that the visceral pleasure of being whipped and slapped and bitten and fucked. Hard."

"Jade!"

"You can't talk about this in any other way than clinically. That's sad."

"I don't want to analyse you. I just…"

"You can't help it. It's your only defence," Jade said. She was getting up to leave.

"I can't do what you want simply because you want me to."

"Why not?" Jade said standing at the table.

"Because it goes against what I interpret as a loving relationship."

"That's limited thinking, Anna. I know you've got more to you than that."

"No," Anna said finally. "If you need to find that experience elsewhere, I would hope that you'd tell me where you're going and with who. And how you're getting there."

"I don't want to go there with anyone else. But I will," Jade said quietly.

"Don't go," Anna said, with just enough authority for Jade to sit back down.

They finished their meal inside a gulf of silence that infiltrated and poisoned their relationship.

A few nights later as they were finishing up dinner at home, Jade said deviously, "I have a present for you, babe."

"Oh yeah?" Anna had an idea of what might be coming.

"Yeah."

Jade came around the table holding something behind her back. She dragged her red fingernails along the edge of the wood. Anna watched her elegant creamy hand. Delicate features and graceful souled, Jade was a fragile woman in some ways. Easy to break. She had hidden horrors in her body that Anna had never probed, but could sense. There was something gone about Jade, something already broken. It was a feature of Anna's attraction to her. She had always been compelled by slightly fractured people. People like Simon.

Jade came around and straddled Anna on her chair. She leaned forward and kissed her on the neck, then on the lips. Jade's mouth waited for a moment on Anna's lips and to Anna it felt like a goodbye kiss. Jade set the bag between them. It rested there between their crotches like a secret waiting to pop open and do something. The bag felt heavy, like it was going to bring damage. Danger. Like it could bring light.

Anna couldn't help in retrospect see that moment, that bag sitting between them as entirely symbolic. And knowing what she knew, the kiss was a farewell to a former way of life.

"This is for you," said Jade. "For us." She lifted up the bag and pushed it towards Anna.

Anna opened the lip of the paper bag and reached in. Her hand around the prosthetic cock and the leather strap.

Jade had tapped into a vein that Anna had tried to keep concealed. It wasn't healthy, Anna told herself, but the voice was weakened by the drum of excitement.

There was a rope. Candles. Lubricant. Flat needles. Each item was retrieved from the bag and set upon the table so that when they were all laid out they looked like ingredients for a hermetic experiment. A leather crop. And an eyeless hood.

When the bag was empty, Anna didn't say anything, and Jade just watched her, with an enigmatic half-smile. Anna studied Jade's face for a long time. She was so lovely. After a moment, Anna began to return each item slowly to the bag and Jade's smile started to fade.

"I can't," said Anna.

Jade simply stared.

Anna lied. She wanted to. Her body was tripped and electric and she wanted to strap on that prosthetic cock and fuck Jade right there against the table. She wanted to watch Jade's body leap and twitch when the red wax from the candle splashed against her flesh. She wanted to slowly luxuriate in tying the knots around her slender ankles and wrists. But she had taken an oath. As a healer, she had sworn that she would never wilfully hurt another living thing. The thoughts that the items inspired individually and together sickened and excited Anna. She told herself that the urge to dominate Jade had came more from feeling manipulated than from an authentic desire to do so.

"I can't," said Anna, this time more to herself than to Jade.

"Yes, you can," said Jade finally.

"No," said Anna and pushed Jade off her lap.

Two nights later, when Jade was sleeping in the other room, the anger finally overwhelmed Anna. The desire to fuck Jade had grown inside her body throughout the past few days. Jade's silence and frigidity only aggravated Anna's fever. She had no objectivity, no patience. She wanted to fuck her, to punish her for putting her in this position in the first place. Anna found the bag of theatre equipment in their closet and she grabbed it. Gripping the paper bag at the neck, she stormed into the guest room.

"You want to know what it feels like to be manipulated, you little bitch," she said to Jade.

Jade rolled over in the darkness.

"Anna…"

"Get up," Anna said quietly.

Jade didn't move. "Anna, I don't want to if you. . ."

"Get up," Anna said again. Her voice quivered, but she did not yell. Jade pulled the sheet away and sat up. She was beautiful, and Anna didn't want anyone else to have her. If she didn't do this, she felt she would lose her. She was too beautiful and too breakable for anyone else. Anna knew what to do with her.

Anna put the hood on Jade and made her kneel in front of her, her cunt wet and her body shaking with excitement. Reduced by the submission, Jade seemed more beautiful than ever.

Anna had wanted to blurt it all out to Simon, but couldn't. Simon was too conservative. And she knew that he absolutely would not approve of her bending the ethics of their profession, even if it was in a personal realm. She also knew that on some level she had enjoyed the secret. She had enjoyed the strange disruption that her games with Jade had imposed on her life. Until St. John came. She ordered another drink.

She had worked hard to keep her relationship with Jade within certain boundaries, but over the last few months the hairline fractures of trouble had become obvious fissures and cracks. Jade wanted to go further and further into the darkness of their games. She wanted to test the limits of endurance and pleasure, and a point was coming soon where Anna knew that she couldn't hold it together. That she would have to say no, and Jade would keep moving into it. Without her.

The dinner party had been a feeble attempt to yank everything back into some semblance of normalcy. She remembered the strain of trying to chat easily with Simon. How lame and posed the whole evening felt. How could she smile and play the artificial hostess when she knew about the bruises and the marks that she had made on Jade's back. It was clear that night that no dinner party or pleasant small talk was going to return her and Jade to where they had once been.

"He could get me a really great book deal, Anna. He's been known to get first time authors phenomenal deals." Jade had told her excitedly that night when they lay in bed together after the party.

"He's wonderful. Don't you think? So weird. There's something positively subversive about him, but he keeps it fashionably hidden. I like that."

Jade had rolled on her side. Her black hair trembled against her thin shoulder. Her voice animated her body. Her face. Anna watched her mouth. Her eyes.

"He's possibly the most intelligent person I've ever met."

Jade was not looking at Anna's face, but just over her shoulder.

"Why do you say he's subversive? I thought he represented mostly mainstream authors."

"You're jealous," Jade said calmly.

"No, I'm just concerned. I want you to be happy. I don't want you to get hurt."

"Why do you say that?"

"I don't know. There's something about him that doesn't feel right to me. Why don't you meet some other agents before you decide about him?"

"Yes!" said Jade. "It's that feeling of discomfort that he arouses in almost everybody. It is so compelling. I don't need to find another agent. I mean if he decides to take me on, I wouldn't hesitate."

Anna didn't say anything. The jealousy settled in her belly and felt like an empty metal bowl.

"I don't know," Jade said, lying back down. Her eyes were still alert. She stared at the ceiling.

Anna reached over and caressed her lover's breast.

"Don't," Jade said.

Anna withdrew her hand as if she'd been bitten. Anna sat up and looked at Jade.

"It's his sexual vibe. There's something about it…" Jade said absently.

"Do you want to fuck him?" The clumsy jealousy slipped out before Anna could check it.

Jade smiled slightly and then she turned her head and watched Anna for a moment.

"No."

Anna laid back and stared at the ceiling. After a while she said, "I'm worried."

"About what?"

"About us."

"You should be," Jade said and rolled on her side, her back to Anna.

Anna ordered another drink, and started to get pissed, but the sentiment lasted less then the length of a cigarette. She put her head in her hands and started to laugh at the absurdity of the situation. She was going to lose her lover because she wasn't beating her in the proper way.

XXI

The Confession

None of the speeches that Lazar had prepared in the cab on the way to the restaurant prepared him for meeting St. John.

"Hello, Dr Lazar," William St. John said. He stood away from the bar and put out his cigarette. He held out his hand and Lazar took it. In touching the man an electric contract seemed sealed.

"Hello, William," Lazar said.

Lazar had expected that some of the feelings that he'd had about St. John were nothing more than fanciful projections. He told himself that when he actually saw the real St. John, he would be reminded of his ordinariness, but he was wrong. The exact nature of St. John's presence still eluded him.

"I'm glad to see you too," St. John said when Lazar smiled.

It suddenly occurred to Lazar that St. John had interpreted their meeting as a possible tryst. He found that he wasn't resisting the idea as he ordinarily would have. Nothing was as it had been.

"Yes. Well, I wanted to…"

"Won't you sit down and have a drink before we go to our table." It wasn't a question. Lazar found a stool and pulled up to the bar. Suddenly he didn't know if he wanted to mention Jade. He wasn't sure he wanted to make clear to St. John that he wasn't here on a social call. He ordered a double.

They sat in silence for a moment and then St. John said, "I know why you're here, and I have to admit that I'm ashamed of my vulgarity."

"You know why I called?" Lazar said stiffly.

"Yes, and I'm terribly embarrassed. I've never done anything like it before. It was just. . ." St. John smiled and shrugged easily. "There it was, and so I put it in." His smile cool but not unauthentic.

Lazar located a sense of righteous anger and held on to it as if it were a life raft inside all this confusion. Lazar leaned forward and said under his breath, "How dare you talk about it that way, you little fuck."

St. John's expression didn't change. He sipped his drink watching Lazar over the rim of his glass.

"You have no idea what you've done," Lazar said, feeling his anger already subside. It wasn't real. "You could have really hurt her," he said, floundering.

St. John looked up quickly. He was genuinely surprised. "Who?"

"Who? Jade! That's why I'm here. I came to tell you to keep your fucking hands off her. You don't know what you're playing with."

St. John looked stricken for a moment. He held his drink aloft and simply stared at Lazar, and then setting his glass on the bar started to laugh quietly. His laughter startled Lazar. It was a sound as equally as ugly as Maya's had been and had the same weird effect coming from a man as handsome as St. John. Lazar was reduced by St. John's laughter. He stood to go. He felt desperate and embarrassed and he wanted nothing more than to get away from St. John. From the city. From everything. He suddenly realised that he had been hoping for a sense of redemption from this meeting. From a stranger, and a sadist.

"Oh, Simon. Please don't go," St. John said composing himself. "Please, forgive me. Oh," he put his hand on Lazar's arm. "Please stay and have dinner. You really don't understand anything, do you?"

His reaction flustered and confused Lazar. The sensation of the man's hand on his arm aroused him in an alarming and foreign way. The vague remembrance of an erotic dream with St. John in it drifted through his consciousness. Having already started drinking earlier in the day, he found he was more drunk than he would have liked to have been. He felt a gnawing sensation that he might start crying again but he didn't even really care anymore. His standard parameters of social and personal decorum were shifting and morphing from minute to minute. He thought to himself that his personality was finally disintegrating. He stood there at the bar, his hands limp at his sides.

"Simon, please sit down. We have a terrible misunderstanding." Lazar sat down.

"*I* was referring to the business card I left in your coat. I was intrigued with you and hoped to see you again. Later, I was sure that I had offended you. That my pithy question at dinner. . ."

"What question?" Lazar said.

"When I asked you if you were a voyeur. I thought I had upset you. But I had already put the card in your coat. When you called, I thought that you were also expressing interest. Apparently not." St. John was too composed. It unnerved Lazar further.

"What about Jade?" Lazar blurted. "What did you do to her?"

St. John looked across the bar for a moment. He turned and leaned over close to Lazar. He could feel St. John's breath on his cheek.

"A pathetic masochist. Really. But then you know what I mean."

Lazar was revolted. He did know what St. John meant.

"Not Jade," Lazar heard himself say without conviction. Everyone was capable of anything. It was the single remaining truth of his profession.

"Oh, yes," St. John said without any feeling. He nodded to the bartender for two more drinks. "Oh, yes."

Lazar found that he was oddly disappointed that St. John had actually engaged in some kind of sexual scene with Jade. He felt jealous and this confused him even further if it were possible.

"Don't ever touch her again," Lazar said blankly, not looking at St. John.

"Oh, I didn't touch her in the first place," St. John said looking at Lazar. "Do you think that I would. . . Oh Simon, we have so much to learn about each other."

Everything was fragmenting and breaking apart in Lazar's psyche. "I don't want to know you," he said numbly.

"Yes," St. John said. "Yes, you do." He looked directly at Lazar and he couldn't stand it. He turned away.

St. John smiled slightly.

"You can't help it."

"Because I'm a voyeur," Lazar said sarcastically.

"Yes, I know. Are you going to stay and join me for dinner?"

Lazar put his head in hands.

"I *am* a voyeur," Lazar said. This time he was serious.

"Yes. You are. But we'll work something out," said St. John. He stood. "Shall we go in?"

Lazar looked at him from between his hands. He raked his

hands through his hair and stood as well. He felt that he simply had to follow the current of this strange breakdown. He felt unable to do anything else.

They didn't talk for the first quarter of the meal. St. John seemed unbothered by the huge silence. Uncharacteristically, Lazar had the compulsion to suddenly fill the space with words.

He inhaled deeply and said, "I would like an explanation about what happened between you and Jade."

"How does that concern you?

"She's my friend. Anna is one of my dearest friends."

"Is this about Jade or Anna?"

"I am speaking to you on their behalf," Lazar said calmly.

"Are you certain?" St. John smiled slightly and put his fork down.

"Of course," Lazar said. "Who else would I be speaking for?"

"Yourself? Or shall we call it your professional curiosity." St. John turned his concentration back to his food. The faint smile on his lips irritated and aroused Lazar.

"You needn't patronise me, St. John. I am simply here — "

"Listen," St. John looked up suddenly. "People do what they do voluntarily. It is my business. It is Jade's business. As far as her mistress...What's her name?"

"Anna?" Lazar said. He was getting a headache. His body hurt. "Her lover's name is Anna."

"Yes, that's right. If she can't keep her pet in line, it is no fault of mine."

"Pet?" Finally something that amused Lazar. He smiled.

"Yes. You find that amusing, I see. I'm sure from your clinical vantage point, masochists and sadists are very amusing indeed. In reality, it is not amusing at all. I guarantee you that." St. John was still focused very seriously on Lazar.

"I don't believe what you're suggesting. Are you telling me that Anna and Jade are into. . ." he stifled a derisive laugh. Yet in the pit of his belly, he knew that St. John was not lying. Yet he could not feature Anna and Jade role-playing some banal fantasy. It was so pornographic, and pornography was not something that he would have associated with either of the two women. But then as he processed the thought, he realised that his sensors and ability to read situations had been impaired for some time. Anything was possible. Nothing was forbidden anymore.

"What happened between my client and myself will remain confidential. I believe that you can understand the necessity for confidence." St. John's expression softened slightly. "You of all people."

St. John picked at his fish lightly with the fork, as if he was mildly disgusted by it, repulsed by the necessity of feeding the body. Lazar remembered his first impression of St. John. Not of the body.

"Well, Anna is very upset," Lazar said lamely after a while. He felt meddling and shamed faced with St. John's composure.

"Why are you?"

"Why am I what?"

"Upset?"

"I'm not upset, I'm just. . ."

"Simon, why are you here?"

"I don't know," he said finally. "I don't know."

"You needed to."

"To what?"

"To see. It's your nature," St. John said serenely.

"No, I don't need to. . . I. . ." Lazar was undone. "I suppose I wanted to see you. I was curious about you."

"In what way?" St. John asked. He was very alert and it was only then that Lazar noticed that he hadn't been drinking any wine or liquor all night. Lazar felt fogged and unclear, but he careened forward anyway. He no longer cared.

"To tell you honestly. . ." Lazar smiled ironically. "I thought you were perverted and it interested me."

"I am perverted. We all are."

"We?"

"You, me. Those women."

"Those women? Do you dislike women?"

"Not particularly, but I really have very little use for them." St. John sat back in his chair and put his napkin on the table. "I do however enjoy collecting their experiences. I enjoy the experiences some of them afford me. I am like you that way. Perhaps our methods differ slightly, but the result is the same. They take us where we need to go. In some ways."

Lazar felt anxious. Guilty.

"Methods. What method do you use?" Lazar said, trying to gain foothold on the conversation. The subtle power exchanges were unnerving him. He definitely felt the weaker opponent in the game. He was unsure of the boundaries and rules quite yet. But he was vaguely enjoying the loss of control.

"I broker my clients' experiences. I broker their voices, their talents, their sicknesses. I sell their insecurities. It's what a good agent does."

"That's absurd," said Lazar.

St. John shrugged. "Just the truth."

"Your truth," said Lazar. He was growing, in equal parts more repulsed and more attracted to St. John.

"Yours too, I believe," St. John replied.

"How do I broker their experiences?" Lazar said.

"Well, money exchanges hands, does it not?"

"Yes, but I don't exploit their experiences once they've revealed them to me." He felt the lie so heavily he almost laughed at himself. St. John laughed instead. It was still a very ugly and unsettling sound.

"Why are you laughing?" Lazar said.

"I don't mind that you hate my laugh," St. John said.

A bolt of electricity powered through Lazar body almost powerful enough to sober him.

"What makes you say that?" he said, immediately on guard. "About your laughter."

"Most people do," St. John said. A thin smile crept across his full lips, waited there and passed. He sat back in his chair and scrutinised Lazar. He waited.

Lazar was suddenly frightened. He felt trapped and confused. He knew the chances of St. John using the exact same words that Maya had said that day she came to his office were very unlikely. Impossible.

"What are you doing?" Lazar said hoarsely.

"I'm having a delightful dinner with an attractive man. What are you doing?"

Lazar hesitated. Maya's name was waiting on his tongue and it seemed as if St. John was coaxing it out.

"What kind of game are you playing?"

"Game? No games. I suppose I should be asking you that," St. John replied coolly. "After all, you did invite me to dinner."

Lazar's mind was clouded. There were too many similarities but not enough information to make a complete link between Maya and St. John. St. John lit a cigarette and watched Lazar through the smoke.

"Why did you fuck with Jade?" Lazar asked.

St. John leaned forward and put his elbows on the table. He spoke softly, "Why are you changing the subject?"

"Why do you represent women writers if you hate them?"

"I don't hate women. I just don't care about them," St. John replied. "Besides my feelings about them have nothing to do with collecting them as talent."

"Why did you mess with Jade?" Lazar insisted.

"Because she wanted me to. Why are you so anxious,

Simon?" St. John smiled.

"I. . ." Lazar was at a complete impasse. "Do you always mix the personal and the professional so blithely?" He said finally. He wanted St. John to cease staring at him so calmly. He wanted the dinner to end, yet he was riveted.

"Yes. Don't you?" St. John smiled ironically at Lazar.

Lazar's anxiety turned to nausea. St. John's smile indicated that he knew much more about Lazar and his "unusual" practices as a physician.

"What do you mean by that?" Lazar said stiffly. He straightened his back and wished he wasn't drunk.

"I think you know what I mean," St. John said dismissively. "Would you like to go somewhere for an after-dinner drink?" St. John said, wiping his mouth. It was the same gesture that he had done at Anna and Jade's dinner party weeks before.

"You aren't drinking," Lazar said suspiciously.

"No, but you are." St. John stood and waited for Lazar to join him.

Lazar had read the signs of danger at dinner, but plodded forward into the experience because, with the exception of Maya's book, this was the most he had felt in years. It didn't matter that the feeling was a dread that invaded his body with every instant he spent in St. John's company.

He felt that there was a subtle form of blackmailing occurring, but he couldn't be sure if it was simply his paranoia or if it was indeed happening. It was too convoluted to be real, and so Lazar had to believe that he had simply lost all rational perspective. He blamed his befuddlement on booze. Or confused sexual boundaries. As he drifted into the fear, he felt a sense of release. When the situation presented itself, Lazar realised that he had been heading in this direction for a long time.

St. John and he stood outside the restaurant and St. John

said, "I think I would like to see where you live. Shall we go to your place?" His voice was neither coy nor suggestive. It was authoritative in an unsettling way. Lazar nodded and hailed a cab. He felt that the less he said, the better until he could formulate some questions that would put him at less risk and reveal more of St. John's game.

The cab ride was pregnant with the silence, yet Lazar's mind was a diuretic cacophony. He began to believe that the whole event with Maya was some kind of set-up that St. John was involved in. He felt duped and betrayed that he had believed her. He had trusted Maya.

Simultaneously, he was having trouble fathoming the charade of his friendship with Anna. He couldn't think about that in the presence of this man. His mind went back to Maya. To the book.

He unlocked the door and let St. John in the apartment. Inviting him into his home forced Lazar to look at his place through St. John's eyes. The rooms looked souless. Pathetic. A clear extension of his mind and body.

St. John made no remark but went and sat on the couch.

"What can I get for you?" Lazar asked. He felt awkward in his body. He felt the anxiety was beginning to show but he was too confused to try and mask it.

"Are you angry?" St. John asked. "Would you like me to go?"

"No," Lazar said, stepping up closer to St. John. He stood in front of him. And then his mind lit on what he needed to do.

"No, forgive me. This evening has just been a little. . . stressful. Would you like something to drink?" Lazar's eyes went down to the foot of the sofa. Near St. John's shoe, he could see the tip of the black journal peeking out from under the couch.

Without saying anything, he casually walked over and picked it up and put it on the table. "I think I'm going to have a port? Would you like one?"

"No, thank you. Perhaps later," St. John replied. He didn't even glance at the journal.

Lazar went into the kitchen and poured the drink. He waited in the kitchen for a long moment, listening. He was sure St. John would at least touch the book. But when Lazar returned, the book was in exactly the same place. His head pounded and he felt his body could not contain the tension any more.

"Why don't we just stop with this now," Lazar said.

"Stop with what."

"I know that book is a phoney and you and she are playing some kind of psychodrama with me. I don't know what you have on me, so we might as well have it out now. It's over, so let's have it. Let's have it." His voice had lifted to a shout and it quivered with unrestrained anger. "What do you have on me? What do you have? Come on," his body was alight with a strange desire for liberation from all his secrets. He had always expected that it would all come down in some kind of uncivilised way. He had hoped for it. He had prepared for it. He thought of the SIG.

"What are you talking about?" St. John's face was so sincerely shocked, that it stopped Lazar instantly.

"That book. . ." He faltered. He wasn't so far gone that he couldn't recognise the first signs of a true breakdown. The paranoia. The persecution. He sat down on the nearest chair, his body giving way.

"You've never seen that book before?" he asked wearily. His gaze fell on the journal. His feelings were completely ambivalent. Betrayal was rank in the room. Yet he didn't know what he owed Maya. He didn't know what he owed anybody anymore.

"What book?' St. John asked, his voice pulled tight from the tension. "I don't know what you're talking about."

"That book, goddamit!" Lazar shouted and pointed at the

journal on the table. "That fucking book! Who is Maya? Who is Maya? Who are you? Why are you doing this to me?"

"Simon," St. John laughed shortly. "I am afraid that I don't know what you mean." He stood to go. "I see that this is obviously not a good time for you. I should just leave you alone." He seemed disappointed and genuinely unnerved by Lazar's bizarre outburst.

It satisfied Lazar to see St. John looking uncomfortable. It gratified him to see that St. John's composure could be cracked, however slightly.

"No, please," Lazar said, after a moment. "I am terribly sorry. I am confusing you with something else. I am just confused about Jade and...you." He looked up from his hands at St. John.

"You needn't worry about Jade, Simon. She's not unhappy," St. John said sitting back down. "Would you like to talk about what's going on, or would you prefer me to leave?"

"Stay. Please."

Somehow confessing about Maya's journal to a near stranger was much easier than telling a friend.

The few steps from the couch to the bed were that much more simple once he had revealed his secret to St. John.

XXII

Crossing Over

When it was all done and Lazar was alone in his room that night, he thought that he should call Anna and tell her. He thought that he should tell her to keep Jade away from St. John. The danger lingered in the room. And the shame. His mind drifted to the .357 in the bureau drawer, and its existence afforded him some consolation.

Even though only a few hours had passed since, he couldn't remember how the events actually unravelled.

Lazar recalled that St. John remained seated on the couch across from him and he seemed comfortable enough to wait for Lazar to talk. There was a long silence while Lazar composed himself.

"That book," Lazar said and nodded towards the journal on the table.

"What about it, Simon?" St. John didn't look at it. "Is it yours?"

"Yes. No. I don't know," Lazar laughed. It was a meaningless sound. "A patient left it behind. Well, not really a patient. A woman who came to see me."

"If you would prefer not to tell me this, I — "

"No," Lazar interrupted. "I need to tell someone. It's just that...well, for a moment I thought that you were actually responsible for me having that book. I know it sounds ridiculous. Of course it *is* ridiculous. I'm just tired. I'm so tired."

"This book?" St. John said, amused. He picked up the journal and started to open it. Everything in Lazar's body rebelled. "No. Please don't read it."

"As you wish," St. John set the book down within arm's reach on the table. He didn't say anything.

"A woman came into my office a few weeks ago... she was very beautiful. And very disturbed. She left that book and I've been reading it."

"Is it good?" St. John said, almost ironically.

"It's not a matter of whether it's good or not. It's just..." Lazar felt foolish yet glad to reduce his feelings to the banality of a confession. "Her pain, her personal suffering, and the way that she describes it, it arouses me. Rather it arouses certain feelings in me." He ended awkwardly.

"What kind of feelings?"

"I can't define them exactly. But the feelings are…" He hesitated. "My feelings are unseemly. Unprofessional."

"So? That must not be an entirely new thing," St. John said.

His words were so loaded with meaning that Lazar tore his gaze from the book.

"Why do you say that?"

"No reason. I just would assume that certain feelings would arise when you are dealing with other people's. . . intimacies," St. John said, the corner of his mouth lifting slightly.

"I am trained to cope with those feelings. Under ordinary circumstances."

"Yes, but you remain human."

"Well, I have been confused about the ethics of holding on to something in such a personal way." He felt he was struggling to bring the conversation back to the book.

"How is it personal?"

"I don't know, but it is. I am worried about the girl who left it. Maybe she left it by mistake and now is ashamed to retrieve it."

"Why should she be ashamed? Obviously some unconscious motivation forced her to leave it. Or lose it. She clearly wanted to leave it with you."

"Yes, but what for?"

"I don't know. To be heard? What does she say about the book."

"She never came back for it."

"Ah I see. What does the book say."

"It's really just about sex. About men she's been to bed with and how she feels about them. But it is having an effect on me…I can't seem to talk about it in any terms that aren't going to sound hopelessly superstitious."

"What kind of effect?"

"I feel as though the book is changing with me as I read it, and I in turn am being changed by the book."

"Books do change in each reader's hand. I'd like to read it."

"Take it," Lazar said suddenly. Once the words were out, he felt the betrayal was complete.

St. John made no move to pick up the book, but instead stared at Lazar for a long time.

"Simon," he said.

The way that St. John said his name, he might as well have said, *I'm going to fuck you.*

Lazar was consumed with an instant sense of grief in having given up the book so easily and the sadness was warped and confused into the moment with St. John. He was being seduced. He hadn't realised what a whore he'd become until St. John made him feel like a prostitute. A voyeur. A pet being willfully manipulated. He was overwhelmed by the chaos of physical and emotional confusion. St. John watched him for a moment and then said, "Undress, Simon."

Lazar didn't move.

"You want to. You wouldn't have called me if you didn't want to. Now, I want you to remove your clothing. I want to look at you," St. John very calmly. His voice had a sense of authority in it that truncated any resistance in Lazar. To his own amazement, he stood and began to unbutton his shirt. His fingers fumbled at the buttons and he realised it had been years since he felt this kind of anticipatory excitement in the presence of a potential lover. It suddenly seemed obvious that he would be undressing in front of St. John, yet when the moment finally came, Lazar was surprised to find that it was not awkward as he would have expected. It seemed like a natural progression of events. He had relinquished his power to St. John by revealing his secret. And in doing so, Lazar realised that it felt good. But he wouldn't feel completely relieved until he had done some kind of personal penance.

The act of fucking another man wasn't the penance; it was the way he got fucked that was the payment. The purgation.

While there was a natural animal drive that propelled Lazar into the situation, the same animal instinct caused Lazar fear. St. John ran his eyes down Lazar's chest, and found the buckle of his belt. Lazar undid the clasp and the sound of the metal hitting the wood floor signalled the crossing.

As he undressed before this stranger, Lazar felt as if he were transgressing an intrinsic personal taboo. The thought made his cock harder and fear sped him towards and carried him through to the final convulsive act.

Once his clothing had been undone, St. John stood and came towards Lazar. He remained completely clothed. His movements were heavy-footed and unreal. Lazar observed what followed through a kaleidoscope of liquor, guilt and confusion. His sensory perception seemed super-attenuated but separated from his body. They were like two events colliding. Two bodies in separate spaces. Entities happening outside of one another. The actions and motions were happening outside Lazar's will, yet he had willfully constructed them. It was as if he were a victim of his own desire. His cock was partially hard and he instinctively covered it with his hand.

"Move your hand away. I want to look at you," said St. John.

Lazar did as he was told and in that moment the roles of their relationship were finally and clearly determined. As St. John looked at him, he felt his cock get harder. The balance of power seemed immutable and unwavering. Whatever happened next was going to be St. John's responsibility because Lazar was ready to be on the other side. He wanted to be the patient, the victim, the lover rather than the loved. He wanted to be on the bottom.

"Get up," St. John said calmly. The tone of his voice was conversational as if they had been at a dinner. He lit a cigarette and waited. Lazar's body felt paralysed and unfamiliar.

"I said, stand up," St. John said again.

Lazar stood.

"Go into the bathroom." Instead, Lazar started to move towards St. John.

It was as though he were holding on to some last vestige of his former self, and he felt compelled to make a final, vain attempt to bridge the power gap. He didn't know what he expected to do when he got closer to St. John and so he simply reached out to touch him.

"Don't touch me," St. John said, standing away. "I prefer

not to be touched."

Lazar turned and went to the bathroom. St. John didn't follow immediately. Lazar could hear him lighting a cigarette and sit back down on the couch. He strained and heard St. John open the book. Lazar's body gave a final twitch and then he fell into the immediacy of the moment.

He waited in the bathroom in the dark for a while and then turned on the light. He looked at himself in the mirror and didn't recognise anything. He turned away and sat on the toilet. He waited more and just as he felt the discomfort of coming back to his body, he heard St. John say from the doorway.

"I sent you in here to wash yourself. What are you doing?"

"I don't know," Lazar said simply. He looked at St. John and waited.

"I want you to clean out your asshole and your mouth. I don't like dirty boys." St. John left the bathroom again, and Lazar mechanically set about doing what he was told. He turned on the shower and began bathing. As he ran his hands over his own body under the spray of the water, his hands felt disconnected and he was searching unfamiliar terrain in the slopes and folds of his body. He was imagining what it would feel like if it were St. John's hands and fingers finding out his body this way.

He got out of the shower and towelled. His erection had not faded and despite the disembodied feeling, he was extremely aroused by the unknown.

He stepped into the bedroom, and found St. John sitting naked on the bed, reading Maya's journal. The rage that such an invasion would have ordinarily caused him was a remote feeling. Lazar observed the situation as outside himself and didn't have any stake in the emotions. His present state was giving into a pure experiential moment. He was leaving language behind.

St. John set the book down. And looked at him.

"Are you clean?"

Lazar didn't answer.

"Good. I'm glad you didn't say yes. Because you're filthy. You're a filthy boy. Come here, you piece of shit."

Lazar came forward. His house, his body were no longer his own.

"Make my cock hard," St. John said.

"I thought you didn't want me to touch you," Lazar said quietly.

"I don't. I want you to touch yourself. I want you to kneel down on the ground right there and put your hands around your cock and make it hard. I want you to get on your knees in front of me. Now."

Lazar did as he was told. He felt a heat flush his chest and neck, and the fire travelled down the centre of his body. When he put his hand around the shaft, he felt the warmth. He started to masturbate and he felt foolish and exposed. He closed his eyes.

"Open your eyes," St. John said. Lazar saw that St. John's cock was hard. St. John's body was sleek. Hairless and defined without being muscular.

"Yes, that's right. I want to see you make yourself harder. I want you to see how it feels to be watched."

Lazar pulled on his cock and it gave him little satisfaction at first. But as he watched St. John's hand move against his own chest, as he watched St. John put his graceful hand around the shaft of his prick, Lazar felt connected to him.

"Get on your hands and knees. When I say, you may come near me."

Lazar understood these games as childish, but was appreciating the obviousness of them in a way that he never thought he would. He fell to his hands and knees, suddenly eager to

please St. John. He wanted to touch him. He moved towards
the foot of the bed quickly. When he got closer, he saw that
St. John had taken a handkerchief from the drawer. He wondered if St. John saw the gun. He waited like a dog at the foot
of the bed.

St. John tossed him the handkerchief. "Blindfold yourself."

Once he had been pitched into darkness, St. John allowed
himself to make contact with Lazar.

The first touch was sudden and frightened Lazar. His body
crackled under St. John's fingertips and he felt a cock nuzzle
against his cheek and then suddenly St. John shoved the
whole member into Lazar's mouth. The smell of pubic hair
and powder filled his nose and the feeling of the flesh against
the inside of his mouth surprised him. His gag reflexes seized
up and St. John grabbed him by the hair. "Suck my cock,
bitch. Don't you pull your mouth away. Suck it."

Lazar opened his throat to take the length of St. John's
prick, and as he did, memories of all the women who he'd
shoved his cock into filled and flooded his memory. He pulled
on St. John's cock with his lips, wanting to take it inside himself. He wanted the memories. He wanted to feel the sadness
and the fear and the shame. The cock inside his mouth was
the first familiar thing that he'd felt in some weeks even
though he had never touched another man in his life. St. John
pulled his head against his belly and pumped his narrow hips
against Lazar's mouth. Quite suddenly he stopped and the
contact between them was instantly severed. Lazar remained
on his hands and knees, his cock pushing downward, the pres-
sure in his balls pressing against the skin. He felt as if he were
inside a fragile moment in which anything could happen.

He felt St. John from behind. St. John spat and put saliva
on his cock and without any teasing of Lazar's asshole, pushed
the entire length of his cock inside. Lazar cried out involun-

tarily and when he did, St. John hit him hard on the ass. St. John continued to hit him as he pumped his cock into the virgin hole. St. John was silent. Nothing more than skin and motion. The pain was terrible, yet Lazar's erection continued to strain. His elbows buckled and St. John pulled him up by the hair. And then, as suddenly and abruptly as it started, St. John pulled his cock out of Lazar's ass hole.

"I thought I told you to wash yourself, you dirty filthy boy." He came around to Lazar's mouth and shoved his cock inside.

"That's right. Clean it up. Eat your own shit and blood. It's what you deserve. I'm actually being too kind as it is."

Lazar was repulsed by his own faeces and blood on the tip of St. John's cock but he opened his mouth and accepted it. He deserved to eat shit.

"That's right, pet. You are an obedient little thing. So obedient. I didn't think you were quite as weak as you are. That's right." St. John was losing his erection. He pulled away from Lazar. Lazar put his hand up to his mouth to wipe it, but St. John grabbed his wrist.

"I've been too kind to you. The least you can let me do is look at you with shit and blood on your lips for a moment before I go." He let go of Lazar's hand and Lazar felt St. John step away.

Lazar was suddenly filled with the urge to cry. His body had not been satisfied yet he didn't think he could tolerate a second caress. He couldn't repress the sound and it came out in a spontaneous long keening which erupted from his shit-stained lips.

St. John laughed at him. He heard St. John putting on his clothes. Lazar was confused. He hadn't come. He hadn't made St. John come. He was humiliated but his desire was still active in his body, the desire was still close to the surface of his flesh. His skin was beginning to welt where St. John had beaten him.

He reached up to pull the blindfold off, and St. John said,

"Leave it on until I'm gone."

Lazar fell back to his knees, crying like a child.

"What happens when the voyeur goes blind?" St. John said and then left Lazar on his knees in the bedroom weeping pathetically.

All the lovers he'd ever had jerked and spasmed through his consciousness. He left the blindfold on for a few minutes after he heard St. John close the front door behind him. He didn't think he could look at himself. He waited until his erection was completely gone, and then he reached up wiped his mouth and took off the blindfold.

Lazar showered and changed the sheets but he was sure that he could still smell St. John on the pillows. He was bereft without Maya's book and he lay awake in the darkened bedroom wondering where he went from this point.

XXIII

Meta-Porn

It's not necessary that I touch them anymore. The slow burn of sado-masochism has driven my evolution. I looked for the pain and it drove the Maya out of the wound easily enough at first. The first contact of whip to ass. The first sustained humiliation that was cloaked in a costume of love. The degrees of love measured in marks, and scars.

I have been scurrying like a rat under night, my scarred belly dragging on the reeking floor of lousy dungeons from New York to San Francisco. The body drunk on power explodes in an orgasm and another manifestation. I changed as quickly as I came. Rat-bodied and wearied by the fading allure of porn, the Maya lived with the theatrically enhanced sexual experience. It was easier to avoid getting touched, but the Maya were still able to find a way out.

Tie me up. Fuck me with that plastic cock. Finger me with your camera. Lick me with the wax. But do not. Do not touch me.

Previous Maya had endured controlled events of pain.
Previous Maya had been born and died in bondage. Under the
knife and needle. Hot wax and verbal abuse. The dungeon
had served as a maternity ward and the Maya had slipped out
under whip and boot. The Maya found that grief, pleasure,
pain or serene detached manipulation can coax out a new
Maya. Fucking is still an effective method, but it is so messy.
All those fluids. All that sweat, saliva and sperm. All the excessive language and costuming. It is not necessary that we touch
any more.

Maya 24 knew that there were other uses for my cunt
besides employing it as a storage space or a scalpel to open the
wound. I found that she could do it telekinetically. I found
that I didn't always need the murderer's cock to finish the
operation. When Maya 24 turned on the telekinesis, we
stepped into the birthing process pornographically. Any one
of our ghosts could come and pull open that scar.

Sex was the necessary component, but that didn't mean that
Maya 24 had to touch anyone. Maya 24 understood autono-
my and commerce. She understood the huge machine of
pornography; that was the function of her manifestation. To
inform the body of Planet Disease's meta mind. Meta-porn.
Literal porn is the purist manifestation of every other kind of
concealed power exchange. Porn is an honest day's work.
Maya 24 understood the bureaucracy of brokering the body's
needs. She was shrewd and had the force of all the other Maya
at her disposal.

Not all the Maya previous had contact with the dead selves.
It took a number of beatings, a series of woundings until finally there was very little pain in accessing the memory of a former manifestation. They were no longer of me, they had
returned to the essential matrix of Maya 30. When the power
of being a masochist waned, the Maya reverted to topping. It

was easier to avoid being touched.

Maya 24 was the first to consciously understand the currency of worldly desire.

Unlike the previous Maya, Maya 24 had the desire to control her own body through the control of others. Humiliating her tricks allowed the telekinesis to kick in. She held the corners of the wound shut until she met her perfect bottom.

Maya 24 had absorbed the pornographic imagination so adeptly that she didn't even need the outfit of a mistress when the right slave came along. It was so much more sinister to dominate him without any coercive props.

St. John lit another cigarette. The sun was coming up and he had been reading the book ever since he had returned home from his dinner with Lazar. He could not yet decipher his feelings about the journal. The revulsion and the fascination were invading his psyche in equal measure.

One thing was certain. It was the first manuscript he had stayed awake through the night to read.

XXIV

Hi & Baptism

I've got it on Channel J. Whenever the watersports advertisement comes on and the bottle blond drinks the fountain of piss (Gatorade) and the voice-over says, 976-PEEE, *the extra e is for extra pee*, I switch it to Trinity Broadcasting. The Jesus Channel. All Jesus, All the Time. When anyone starts crying out of gratefulness to the Lord, I switch back to Channel J.

I have one more day before it comes down. Writing this last with a .357 to my head. I have waited. I have been patient with the absurdities and the filigree of the monkey mind. I have written most of it down before the 29th. Some say the last is the hardest, but it gets easier. It's a slide into home, though it is true that the most recent seem harder to fictify. Harder to diddle the memory. Thinking about all the Maya still makes the wound ache and itch. But soon I will be inside the 30th. Free. Quieted. Liberated from the extra pee. Jesus-free. The nastiness of the body won't even be a memory. And the dull throb of the wound will cease. One more day.

The smack and grind of leather and skin, the pseudo groans still sound tracking my scene even though all the other Mayas are dead. Whores all. Magdalens for the money. The costuming and smells are the remnants from the continual porno loop of Planet Disease. The ambition to climb out of the noise and flesh is only recent.

Maya 27 died mid-ritual, offering herself in front of a bored audience. A TV-lit living room in the Mission of San Francisco. The whole soul death is imprinted on tape. It's so much more indestructible, yet more disposable than a photograph. Photographs steal your soul, videos just kidnap it for a while. We sold this one to some visiting Japanese salarymen who would have preferred some extra pee. We gave them blood instead. It would have to do. Cash on delivery.

The pull into porn is too strong to avoid. It is pure velocity. It is as pervasive as Coca-Cola advertisements, and Maya 27 had been following the lead of previous manifestations, a series of suicides feeding the carnivorous cum machine. We built our cosmology on the money shot.

I had gone through this scene before, but tonight the angel-winged lysergic acid diethylamide sped the birth, broke the water and flooded the set. By the time we wrapped it up, I was Maya 27. Whipped and cut, pierced and fucked.

While one of the technicians set up the Hi 8 camera, I took the acid jewels from the vial around my neck. It didn't take long for the first chimera of the hallucination to start. I sat very still while the machine moved in its slither around the house. They ignored the performers. Too personal to talk before you get fucked.

She came into the bathroom and said. Have you showered?

I said I couldn't remember back that far. I had been in the bathroom for years.

I hate smelly pussy. You better wash.

My pussy doesn't smell.

Get in the shower anyway.

I got in there and she said her name from the other side of the plastic curtain. Then she changed her mind and said that her name was something else. Shave your cunt, she said, while she applied her mascara. I did it and as I pulled the razor over the soft fold I nicked a little spot. I giggled, thinking of the amount of blood that was going to pour out later on.

What's funny.

I nicked myself.

You're going to be the bottom tonight, she said, ignoring my laughter which had turned almost hysterical. I stepped out of the shower and watched her put on her porn persona.

She was an apathetic pixie until she put on the uniform of cruelty and then she was transmogrified into a daughter of Morgana. Witch born. Childhoodless. She was a dead girl who could kill with a fingernail if she wanted.

I said, I'm Maya. I didn't tell her 26. Too personal.

Are you cool with bottoming? We could switch. I don't care.

Better to have a dominatrix midwife to usher the new manifestation in than a doctor. There would be no hysterics when Maya 27 decided to turn out. She looked to be a fine technician; as skilled as a psychiatrist without all those problematic ethics interfering. She was free of such static. Her bodily noise was a constant tense growl. When she was done dressing, she stood before me, a menacing teenaged psychopomp shining in her Latex shields.

Horse-whipped, black-nailed and cat-o-nine tailed, she said, and stuck her ass out.

She intended to stand by my side when I kicked off. She would drag the carcass away and feed privately. But not until we got it on tape. We were here to make some green.

So you're bottoming tonight? she said again.

I stood there transfixed. Naked. I covered my wound with my hands. She didn't seem to notice, or to care about it. She was more interested in her effect upon me. She scared me. I had never been so close to another dead girl. The bathroom tile breathed. I wondered how many suicides were staged in that bathroom. ODs. Razors. Botched attempts. Tragicomic fuck ups. I started to laugh again and it hurt the wound. I tried to stop but the wound was laughing on its own.

I'll make you stop that laughing, she said. Method action. She was getting into the role.

I let her put on my face. Tarting me up. Elevating me to the proper status.

Is there anywhere you don't want me to hit you? she asked, brushing rouge on my cheeks. I was starting to look like a doll. I couldn't see the contours of my face anymore, just the dolly hole of my mouth.

The face, I said. Don't hit my face. If you hit my face, I'll kill you.

The gory reality of two bitches trying to work out a compromise.

OK, she said easily. What about your pussy? I hate it when anyone smacks my pussy.

Yeah. Don't hit my pussy.

I want you to stay away from asshole. Around it is OK. But that's it. I don't let anyone touch my asshole.

What about fisting?

That's OK. You?

Yeah. Fine. Just use enough lube. How do I look?

Good. Let me fix your lips. Is the acid kicking in?

Just now.

We stepped out of the bathroom. Our arms touched and I felt the scintillating moment of real attraction. It fizzled when the camera man said: OK. Here they are. We got sound?

The room was warm from the lights. Four poster bed. Grubby sheet. Some whips jerry-rigged to the wall. Standard porn backdrop.

Let's get started, ladies, someone said. Time was doing its trick. I felt I had been here all my life.

What's the scenario? she asked. I squinted at her breasts pushed into the latex, I could see through her shirt and skin into body. Her phosphoric ribs. Her hollow flat belly. A maw of a cunt with an iron grip. Bear-trap teeth. Devil tongue clit.

OK, girls. Let's go.

Went to the bed and stood there awkward. I giggled and pulled nervously at the skin of the wound.

Mellow out, she hissed.

I bit the laugh off. Everyone hates my laugh.

Is the camera on? someone said. There was movement in the shadows. The smell of latex and powder. Pussy.

Yeah. Red light. OK. Rolling.

Her face twisted. The lunar pull of the red light transformed her soft jaw and full lip into a lupine snarl. Her retractable claws came out. The cruelty made her smell different. She didn't have to act. She was the real deal. 100 % dead girl bitch.

You've been a very bad girl, she said.

You have no idea, I thought.

Shine my boots, you dirty little scab.

Maya 26, the great liberator, knelt in front of the maiden dominatrix and shined the boot with her tongue. My mind wandered to Jesus Christ. To the feet of the Buddha. To Mary Magdalen. To the holy whores. Mary washed his feet with her hair. I realised then that Maya 26 and all the former Maya had been looking for God in the money shot.

A series of trite porn rondeaus recurred like a purgatorial round. Pseudo-lesbian tongue touching. No kissing. Taboo. A slap on the ass. More, till it stings. Oh yeah, I said.

False. Liar. Philistine, cried Maya 27 making her entrance on my scene.

This is the last one, Maya 26 countered. The last necessary one. Blowing away all this vinyl between me and the fractal godhead. The chaotic domina goddess. The last one and then we're going straight into the eye of the psychosis where we belong. Where it is safe and muted from this sharp and jagged world. I will deliver us into the wound for good.

The psychopomp took me by the hair and tied Maya 26 to the rod iron bed post. Legs spread. Arms outstretched.

Oh my God, why has Thou forsaken us?

Elaborate knotworks. The lights tanning her back. Ass. The horse-hair whip. Carrying the cross of the sexually liberated. Like a gladiator drunk on the theatre of the crucifixion, my psychopomp brought out her German implements. A tinkling of stainless steel. The scalpels and pincers and speculums clinked onto the bed. She clamped the hemostats onto the nipples. Instruments of the Passion. Blindfold. Gag. Bad girl. You've been a bad girl. She took the scalpel in her little girl fist. She stomped her feet and said, You've made me very angry. Very angry.

When she cut me open, she bent her head over my chest and licked the steady thin stream of blood. Her hair smelled plastic. She said under her breath. Your blood's filled with poison. It's going to make me trip that much harder. No prophylactic between me and it, the wound finally bloomed like a rabid flower. The opening did not occur because of the psychopomp's manufactured caresses. It was not any of the Instruments of the Passion, the cameras, the crops, the needles or the audience. It wasn't the imitation sadism or the faked moans.

I opened my own body through the telekinesis, the power that finally joined mind and body, body and mind. Releasing control had forced the two to finally meet. Maya 26 peered from the edges. She was the seductress that was going to deliver me into the romance of insanity.

She opened the other arm, letting all the artificial light into the body.

The Via Negativa.

I was plunged into the centre of the darkness. Purity in porn. I breathed the heat of a cleansing fire. Baptism. She methodically put the needles in an aureole of piercings around the crown of my nipples. My arms lost all feeling. My legs felt nothing. I was nothing but the wound. A black hole. Antigravity in the cunt. Breast imploding. Heat radiated out to the corners of the room, splashing aortal venom on the set. She lubed her fist and without drama rammed it inside the pink dwarf dead star of my previously owned cunt. The rage of the body responded. The snatch bit. Amputation of desire. She pulled out her bloody stump, leaving her silver ringed hand inside the cunt-corpse of Maya 26.

The video crew took a smoke break. Low voices. Back to work. When she put her face between my legs, the vortex pulled her in. Pushed her face up against the wet flesh until it was satisfied. Still, it was factory work. I had located infinity inside the repetition of the porn machine.

Don't stop now. This is the last necessity, Maya 26 said.

The wound, wider than ever before, coughed up Maya 27. She unfurled just before the money shot and claimed the body victorious. She pushed the fading cadaver of Maya 26 towards the Stanislavski orgasm and then cast her aside. The perfected industry of porn would endure without her.

The carcass of Maya 25 was behind the set, crucified on her rubber dick. The remaining body all odd angles and welts. Food for the psychopomp.

I realised that night that Maya 27 was going to stay curled

around the madness until 30. Until the end of the nagging insults of these personalities.

I smell Armageddon, were Maya 27's first words.

Leave her alone. She's still tripping, said someone else. I waited in the corner until I could walk.

When I re-entered Planet Disease, the music in the other room was tearing my clothes. The psychopomp whore was fucking her usual boy trick pimp up the ass with the juices of Maya 26 lubing his tight poop shoot. A few voyeurs stood around the edges of the circus ring admiring their star's categorically bizarre exhibitionism. Practised perversions. She was a real pro. She stood and pissed on the trick. He opened his maw and took more. The extra e is for extra pee. An empty guitar case sat open near the side of their toiling bodies, ready to accept any gratuity for their sexual depravity. Take photographs please. Please. Something to remember me by. The blue hole video was on a loop and the girl on the porno TV station was saying over and over, "I like my new cock. I like my new cock," rubbing the latex penis with great affectation.

A wall-eyed he-she from Esta Noche asked me to dance when a salsa song came on. We moved clumsily around the bodies on the floor. I could sense that real time was under her dress. The video crew were drinking beers. I wanted to see what was under her dress, and when I got close I could smell the crack perfume in her hair.

One of the full-time voyeurs stepped in. His pronounced limp was made more graceful by the he-she's command of the situation. She took him in her arms, and the two danced a crooked waltz on the carpet of the rental living room. They opened their romance by sharing hits from the pipe and not wiping the mouth piece before letting the other lick it. When I got ready to go, the full-time voyeur had graduated to participant perv and shoved his head under the he-she's dress. A cocksucker before a kisser. The world turned around the money grind. The psychopomp was in the other room, having trussed her boy-trick with hospital tubing. The surgical instruments were near. The leeches, the blood bowls. The spring lancet. A growing stain on the carpet under his left arm. Strange caterwaul of psychic detritus coming from a blasted boom box. Old shit. Tired shit. Fashion. Religion. I was too close to tell what kind of ritual was being performed.

I feel the apocalypse in my bones, I said to them while they fucked on the floor. Someone handed me a wad of bills and I turned and left, drifting onto Mission Street, looking for a place to wait out the final manifestations. The final storms would be weathered alone with all the men in Maya. The self-ishness of madness closed around my shoulders. Wrapping me. Cloaking the wound. I don't need to touch them any more.

XXV

Telephone

Even though St. John had smoked the last cigarette, he kept reading. When he finally arrived at the last pages, he was amazed. Maya had done a quite a good job. He waited until business hours and then started making the calls.

"Yes. This is William St. John. I have just come across a very intriguing manuscript... the author? Well, you see, that's why I'm calling you personally. There is a very fascinating story that is attached to this manuscript. I think we could do some very interesting business with this one. Lunch tomorrow? Fine. That sounds very good."

He hung up. He couldn't be bothered with finding cigarettes.

"Yes, hello. This is William St. John. May I speak to..."

By noon, he had arranged four meetings with major publishers. The first was dinner that night. He showered. Went out and bought a pack of cigarettes and upon coming home made two more phone calls.

Lazar wanted to call Anna, but the ache had him pinned to the bed. He had heard about this kind of depression; he had treated it in others many times, but it was no consolation. Instead of calling Anna, he let his mind fix on the .357 in the drawer. That was a much greater source of comfort than any other feature of his life.

Anna watched Jade sleeping. She knew it was all over and the stink of a dead relationship was already smelling up the apartment. She wanted Jade out of the house. She didn't feel much of anything except the hangover from the night before. She had decided to deal with most of the confusion after Jade was gone. She reached over and tapped Jade's shoulder. She woke and they looked at each other for a long time. Their relationship was unmistakably over.

Catherine Lazar answered the phone. When she heard St. John's voice she smiled. She listened to him for a long time, and then said, "I knew it would work."

When she hung up, she looked out the window for a long time, thinking that the satisfaction should have been more exhilarating. It was only really the beginning, she reminded herself. The beginning of his end.

When the phone rang, the bell tore through his body. The sound was almost more damaging than a bullet. He surprised himself by answering it. He rolled over on the bed. Speaking caused him physical pain.

"Yes."

"This is William," St. John said.

Lazar didn't say anything.

"Are you there? Simon?"

"No."

"Oh, come now. What's the matter?"

"I made a mistake."

"About us."

"There is no us. About the book."

"About the book?"

"Yes."

They waited. Lazar gripped the receiver so tightly that sweat formed on his hands.

"I never finished reading it. I need…" Lazar choked on the words. He felt a vague hint of foolishness flower and then die. There was no soil for any feeling to take root.

"I did finish reading it. It was — " St. John didn't finish the sentence.

It was cruel and Lazar knew that was St. John's intention. He wanted to know what St. John had read. He wanted to know what someone else thought of the journal, yet simultaneously he thought of someone like St. John and how he would interpret it. He was driven to know how her last pages finished but he couldn't bring himself to ask. In some ways, Lazar was convinced that the book had a different ending for each person who read it. He didn't want to know the ending that St. John had read.

Lazar mustered the courage to say, "I want it back."

"I'm afraid I can't accommodate you, Simon," St. John said.

Lazar listened to him exhale the smoke. He was helpless again. "Why?"

"Well, I am phoning to tell you that I intend to sell the journal when I find the right publisher and — "

Lazar sat straight up in bed. Strangers pawing her. Fingers going over her body, searching her words for meanings that weren't there. There wasn't anyone that could possibly understand her the way he did. He couldn't bear the thought of strange eyes projecting false ideologies on her. The book was his.

"You can't do that, St. John. It's my book."

"Certainly, I can," her replied calmly. "It's not your book."

"That journal belongs to my patient. It's confidential. It's a breech of. . . You can't. . ."

"Now, Simon. You really don't have much bargaining power. Do you? Or are *you* going to give me a lecture about medical ethics?"

Lazar could tell that St. John was smiling.

As Lazar suspected, St. John had something incriminating and imminently concrete on his misbehavior as a psychiatrist. By the certainty in St. John's voice, it was something *very* incriminating. God knew there were enough women wandering the city that he had "treated".

"I will have the AMA after you so quickly you won't know what hit you," said Lazar. It was a completely empty threat and they both knew it. Lazar was too outside himself to even feel stupid. The words didn't mean anything, but he still wanted the book back. He knew he wouldn't get it.

St. John laughed at him. Lazar pulled the phone from his ear unable to tolerate that horrible sound. "Please Simon, don't you think that the AMA would be interested in some of your more, how shall I put it, some of your more *modern* practices. Especially with your female patients."

At first, Lazar's mind was in a panic and almost as suddenly as it overwhelmed him, the calm reflooded his body. He lay back against the pillows. This conversation had thrust him through to the other side. He now really knew how she felt. He closed his eyes and let Lazar die. It was the first sense of clarity that he had felt in years. A state of grace descended. He watched the former Simon Lazar fold inside. He felt the wound. Already he knew what it would feel like.

"Simon, you are going to co-operate with me on this, or it will get very unpleasant. Now, here is what I intend to do…"

Lazar gently replaced the receiver in the cradle. St. John's voice went into the drift with everything else.

When Anna heard his voice on the phone, she stiffened and waited.

"I'd like to speak to Jade please."

"You fucking bastard," Anna said.

St. John merely laughed.

"Jade, please."

Anna handed the phone to Jade. They were sitting at the kitchen table where they had been half-heartedly dissecting the corpse of their love for the past hour.

"It's St. John."

Jade took the phone. She didn't bother to go into the other room; there was no point now.

"Yes," Jade said. She listened to St. John.

Anna watched her face. Jade's expression went from neutral to despairing and then bottomed out into an apathetic mask. She didn't say anything else to St. John but "Yes", again and again. In a matter of moments, the conversation was over. She hung up.

She sat down again at the kitchen table and started to laugh. It was a sickening laugh, empty of joy. Empty of meaning.

"I'm a worthless piece of shit," she said. She started to cry. Anna waited. Jade started rocking. "I'm shit. I'm shit. I'm shit."

"Stop it!" Anna said sharply. She couldn't stand the disintegration any more. She couldn't stand her own helplessness. "Stop it," she cried, but Jade kept up the autistic mantra.

After a long time, Jade finally stopped and said dully, "He said that he's going to be representing a new author and there would be a conflict of interest. He said that I wasn't exactly right for him after all. My *style* wasn't exactly what he needed."

"Jade. I'm really sorry. But I think it is really for the — "

"Shut up," Jade said dully, not looking at Anna. Her thin arms were wrapped around her own shoulders.

Anna watched her and realised that she didn't love her enough. That she didn't want to go where Jade was going. They remained seated at the table and the feeble mourning happened in thick silence. Jade finally got up and went into the bedroom. Anna heard her put some clothes in a bag and then listened as the front door closed behind her.

After a while, Anna got up and poured herself a drink.

XXVI

The Wound Tattoo

*t*he shop had the smell of a hospital, an odour that she was familiar with. A hive sound of the tattoo guns filled the small shop with warmth. Heavy metal on the boom. Easy chatting. Bleeding. Weeping sores. Life and death happening. Encapsulated and controlled confrontations of mortality.

This is going to be with you until you die. Forever.

The tattooists bent over their clients delivering the light. Angels with ink. Little annunciations delivered in an irritation of pain.

Rock of Ages. Love Birds. Skulls. Daggers. Roses. Devils. A lot of demons here.

There was a fear of empty spaces that she could relate to. The walls were covered in flash. Crazy pictures. The walls were crawling with beautifully vulgar scars.

I want a tattoo, she said to the guy behind the counter.

What do you want? he said, bored.

She reached into her bag, retrieved the drawing. It unfurled down her front.

He whistled. Christ.

I want you to stencil it on just like this, she said.

Where do you want that thing? He seemed sceptical. A couple of the other tattooists looked up, like gargoyles distracted from their diabolical doodling. The tattooist looked over his shoulder at the guys. As if to say, are you diggin' this bitch? She wants *that* on her body. They thought they'd seen it all.

I want it here, she said.

She pulled the drawing up to her chest. The picture started just below her clavicle and went to a mark just above her pussy.

Do you have any other tattoos? he asked.

No.

I can't do *that* for your first tattoo. Why don't you start with something a little more…something a little smaller. And if you like it, I could —

No. I want this.

I don't think —

I can pay this much. She reached into her bag and removed bills. A couple thousand by the looks of it.

Wait here, he said. He took the drawing with him.

He went over and conferred with one of the other tattooists. They kept looking at the drawing and back at her.

She was ready to go to another shop. She didn't care who did it, just that it got done.

The tattooists talked for a while more.

He came back. When do you want to do this?

Now.

He couldn't deny her confidence. He couldn't deny all that cash.

It's going to be two thousand.

A guy who was getting a tattoo on his arm snorted out loud.

Only a rube would pay two thousand dollars for that tattoo.

Do it now, then, she said.

What's your hurry? I mean, maybe you'll want to think about it. This is a pretty big piece of work. You're not going to like how it feels.

Yes, I will.

Well, let me check my schedule, he said, and went away again.

The buzz in the shop had changed dramatically since she walked in. Both tattooists and those getting operated on were watching the exchange. There was a tension that was growing into a vague, almost sick excitement. She was asking him to mutilate her and they would be circumstantial witnesses.

OK, the tattooist returned. I guess we could start it now. I don't know if I can do it all in one sitting. And it's not going to feel so good on your stomach so why don't we —

I can't come back, she said. Do it today, or not at all.

He was growing intrigued. Now he wanted to do it. And though she was being extremely direct, she wasn't being a cunt. He was starting to like her weird way.

OK. Let me go trace this… he stopped. He didn't know what to call the drawing she had handed to him.

She sat on the other side of the counter and waited patiently while the tattooist drew the picture on some stenciling tissue and then prepared his needles. He pulled out a table and put a Japanese screen around the table.

You want to step around?

She stepped behind the screen. He was unnerved by her eyes. Flat, but not drugged or unalert.

You been drinking? 'cause I can't tattoo you if you have.

No, she said taking off her shirt. I don't drink.

OK. He could tell she didn't want to talk.

Her breasts were nice. Not big but spacious enough and her belly was slightly rounded just above the pubis. Her clean skin turned him on, and he felt a twinge of sadness when he put the stencil down the middle of her.

Why don't you check in the mirror to see if you like the placement.

She looked down at the drawing on her chest and belly.

I don't need to. It looks right.

Are you sure you don't want to just —

No. Why don't we start?

OK.

He put on the rubber gloves and she climbed on the table. She lay down and her black hair spread against the table like an ink blot. He pushed the pedal with his foot. The gun sparked and hissed.

You ready?

She nodded.

He squared his shoulders and leaned over her. He pulled the delicate skin taut just below the little cup of her neck between the clavicle. He took a deep breath and made the first line. She didn't move at all.

What's your name? he said after a few minutes.

Maya.

They didn't talk during the rest of the session. They didn't need to. He scarred her for life without even kissing her.

XXVII

SIG Narcissus

Moving through the room was no longer difficult in his new body. Lazar retrieved a piece of paper from the desk in the other room. The pen in his hand felt completely foreign, the house not his own, and the body that moved from space to space nothing but a gossamer sack that was motivated by a singular thought.

He wrote to the only one who he cared about anymore. It didn't matter that she was probably dead.

Maya, thank you for setting us free. I have at last known love. Died for love. I hope you have too. Yours, Simon.

The period at the end of the sentence is the last good bullet.

He drifted easily into the bedroom and went to the dresser. He watched his hands with a curious amusement. The clarity was soothing and a great relief. When he picked up the gun, he knew that he was doing exactly what was necessary. The cowardice that had been dogging him for years slipped away.

He loaded the gun and went to the bed. He sat down on

the edge with the .357 on his lap. The dreams that he had for the last few weeks flitted through his mind. He thought vaguely of Catherine. For some reason he remembered their wedding and how foreign was that nuptial hope. He felt nothing emotional. His memories were a series of pictures of someone else's life. The fact that these images were wafting through his mind was as though whatever remaining survival mechanism in his body was rebelling. As though his memory was trying to seduce him into living, but none of the thoughts or reminiscences took root. The gun was heavier than he remembered, or his body had just become so much lighter.

When Anna was drunk enough, she tried to phone Simon. It rang and rang. No answering machine. She paged him and got no response. She cried and drank some more. She wandered around the apartment. She wanted to burn the place down. She went to the bedroom closet and pulled out all the equipment that she and Jade had used to prop up their sexual life over the past few months. She took the harnesses and the dildos and the butt plugs. The wrist and ankle restraints and lastly the hood. Holding them as though they contained the plague, she went to the garbage shoot in the hall and threw them down into the incinerator. She rang Simon again and when there was no answer, she went down into the street and got in a cab. She had to tell someone. She had to confess.

"Believe me," said St. John. "This manuscript is going to be the hottest thing this year."

"Who's it by?" the publisher asked, trying to remain unimpressed. But it was after all, William St. John, and he had a habit of making authors.

St. John could tell by the expression in the publisher's face that he wanted it already.

"Well, it's very intriguing story."

"Oh, yes?"

"You see, I came by this manuscript in a very strange way. It has an integral relationship in how we would market a book like this. I'm telling you, Robert, this thing will set the publishing business on its ear."

"Where did you get it?"

"Well, you see, there are certain aspects of the story that I'm not quite yet at liberty to tell. But I came by this book through a psychiatrist. A woman happened into his office. A deranged woman. A beautiful woman. And she left it behind. She'll never come back to claim it."

"How do you know?"

"She committed suicide."

"Oh!" The publisher's eyes lit up. "But isn't that against the ethics of the profession?"

"Well, yes it is. That's where it gets interesting. . . you see this doctor, well he's since started to fall onto some difficult times. *Mental difficulties.*"

"Ah, I see. Well still — "

"There's more to it. . ."

By the end of dinner, St. John knew that he was going to be able to create a bidding war for this silly little journal.

He had already named the book:

Maya 29.

The drive to tell Simon everything was almost pathological.

When he didn't answer the door, Anna decided to get the super to open the front door for her. She told the him that she was Simon's girlfriend and she had left some important work papers in the apartment. The super reluctantly unlocked the front door and followed her inside. She wanted the old man to leave her alone in the apartment, but when she went in the room and found what Simon had done, she was glad that she was not alone with all his blood on the walls.

Catherine Lazar was thinking about the girl that St. John spontaneously produced to play their Maya. The girl who wrote the journal. St. John had never elaborated as to where he had found her or what he had told her in regards to sending her to Simon's office that day, except that he had told her what to say based on how Catherine had described Lazar's most likely reaction to such a situation.

"How do you know she won't come forward when we finally get the book published and say that she was involved," Catherine asked St. John, when they had started planning this over six months prior.

"She won't," St. John had said with great conviction. He rolled to the other side of the bed and lit a cigarette.

"Yes, but how can you be sure of that, William?"

"Her only desire is to please me."

"And where did you meet this domesticated little pet?" she said as they lay in bed together.

"She belongs to me. That's all you need to know," he said.

"If we are really going to do this, I want to know that there are no loose ends."

"OK, Catherine," St. John turned and looked at her. "But you are not going to understand this. Now or ever."

She was visibly offended.

"There is no need to be put off, darling. It is something that only a true masochist can comprehend."

"What do you call me?"

"A dilettante."

She didn't want to argue. How could she not sound ridiculous arguing the authenticity of her masochism. She kept her mouth shut.

"Well," she said after a while, " I think you can tell me how you know that she won't fuck you over when the book comes out."

"She belongs to me. Body, soul and mind."

"How is that possible?"

"Catherine, you can't understand this, but I'll try to explain it simply. When she became my slave, she was granted one request. I asked what she wanted. She said that she wanted me to kill her."

"What?" Catherine snorted. "That's absurd."

"I have never loved a woman more than in that moment."

The fear grew in Catherine's body. She knew instinctively that he was telling her the truth. With him, she was learning that anything was possible.

St. John turned and looked at her. "Yes, my dear. Anything."

Catherine and St. John didn't have a sexual relationship after that conversation. It died a discreet death that both of them realised was shrewd. Not only was he dangerous, but Catherine realised that her potential drive towards being on top was going to keep them in a perpetual inbalance. They worked so much better when they were functioning as mechanical twins with a mutual goal. The Maya 29 Project.

What they called the Maya 29 Project had started as a ridiculous scheme conjured over a bottle of wine and a series of speculative fantasies. Catherine and St. John had met at a party and there had been instant attraction. They agreed to meet again, and St. John found that Catherine had an aptitude for pain. They thought that their relationship was going to be strictly sexual when in actuality it was the recognition of a compatible cruelty.

When they got to know each other even more intimately, Catherine confessed her driving desire to exact revenge on Simon for all the humiliations she had endured during their marriage. St. John was intrigued by the situation and had convinced her that merely reporting him to the AMA would be so unsatisfying. So banal.

"Don't you want to hurt him in the same way that he hurt you?" St. John had asked. "Here," he pointed to his head. "Don't you want to hurt him here?" His index finger remained on his temple.

"Yes," she said.

After Simon shot himself, she thought about that conversation with St. John quite a lot.

XXVIII

Bestseller

After Simon Lazar killed himself, marketing *Maya 29* was seamless. Of course, his suicide had been an unexpected turn of the screw and St. John fretted at first that Catherine would crack under the strain or guilt. But she held up. She maintained that they were already in it this far and he was a stupid fucker for shooting himself.

Besides, once Simon was dead they were to able use him as a solid armature to hang the whole phoney narrative of *Maya 29* on. There were some sceptics in the business because the story was so strange, but when the story was put to the press, the public devoured the intrigue. The hype grew surrounding the strange case of Maya 29, the faceless girl who wrote the obscene journal. The unknown girl who had driven a successful psychiatrist to suicide. The press searched for Maya, but there was no way to find her. Simon's death, and the note he left seemed to validate the journal's authenticity, along with the initial record of her office visit. But there was an aura of mystery, of lies and intrigue that surrounded the book and the publishers and St. John worked that angle tirelessly. By the time the book got to the stores there was enough curiosity to make the media hype and the investment payout. The fact that the text was so unsavoury only added to its appeal. There were threats of bans which made St. John and the publishers gleeful. Possible censorship could assure a couple hundred thousand extra sales. Besides that, whenever there was a tangible tragedy or gory death linked to a book, publishers could be sure to satisfy their public.

Media bit down with titanium fangs and tore out the living jugular of her memory, of his memory, until Maya and Simon Lazar were nothing but a series of vignettes sensationally eviscerated.

Anna didn't understand the note that Simon had left until the book was published. The press that surrounded *Maya 29* was phenomenal and it explained more about what had actually happened with Simon, with St. John, and Jade than Anna wanted to know. Her mind simply could not process the possibility of such unbelievable duplicity and so, she shoved whatever sickening inklings she had about the whole puzzle deep under the skin. She thought that she had seen the worst go by after Simon shot himself and Jade left. Now, whenever she passed a bookstore, she saw the cover. A picture of a lovely girl with black hair and a scar running up the middle of her torso, with big print underneath:

MAYA 29

She found herself thinking of the note over and over:

Maya, thank you for setting us free. I have at last known love. Died for love. I hope you have too. Yours, Simon.

The period at the end of the sentence is the last good bullet.

XXIX

Planet Disease

When I saw St. John, I knew that he was the final one. Previously I hadn't believed in a singular focus of desire. Before him, I hadn't believed in pure desire at all. But the way he carried his body. The way that he committed acts of manipulation and cruelty were poetic and beautiful. I knew.

My mistress at the time offered me to him. She said, Maya, go to Mr. St. John and do what he says.

Yes, I said. I hid my excitement, yet my body was like a piano wire strung across a freeway. Taut, ready for the accident.

That first night he put this body through such paces, I thought that certainly I would break under him. The fact that he refused to touch me but forced other slaves to service his bidding on my body made the pleasure that much more pure. He would not allow me to touch him either. Instead, he watched the scene carefully and made sure his pets attended to my needs as any good sadist will do with a new pet. A pussy like me.

I had been waiting for him for five years. I had taken the beatings, the enemas, the needles, the ropes and fists in preparation for what he would bring me. Ultimate perfection. Delivery.

The night that I was passed from my mistress to him, he chose to brand me. Before he did thus, he asked me if there was anything that I wished from him. He would only ask once.

Kill me.

I had waited too long to say the words and they fell from my lips like fruit almost rotten from ripeness.

The way that he looked at me, I knew then that he loved me and would accommodate my wishes.

At first, I thought that it would be a simple act. He would simply bleed me slowly until the body was drained of senses and plasma and Maya 29 would be gone. This Maya; this chimera of the illusory world reflected in the faulty glass of all eyes. But his way has been so much more subtle. He has killed my name and raped my personality. He has murdered me publicly and I am forever grateful. Set free.

The whole murder of the self has been our delicate construction and I have been a willing architect.

St. John built all the gaudy decorations around my armature. He wrote in all the pathology. All of it. He even gave me the money for the wound tattoo and sent me to do it before I went and saw Simon Lazar.

St. John said that my cunt was nothing but a gaping wound but that I should not bandage it, but wear it for everyone to see as such. I did what he asked. He ordered me to write about my life. My sex. My body. And I did what he asked. And then, finally, St. John told me to go and to never come back. He knew that the worst punishment a sadist can mete out to a masochist is to say *no.*

Of course, I did everything he has asked and now I am dead.

Every time I walk down the street I see my corpse in the bookstores and I realise that I no longer exist. I am without the former boundary of the ego. I carry the body of the all the dead Maya hanging from my side. She is an atrophied twin that cannot be severed but must remain a corpse attached just below the rib. But *I* am no more, because *she* is no more and I am free.

XXX

Preface

What follows is a living book of death. Disease. Death and violence seems to emanate from its pages, though the voice is alive with the pain of mental illness. The strange circumstance that brings this book to print is tragic, misguided and, alas, ends in death.

This book is Maya's story. It is Simon Lazar's story. The actual journal came into my possession from a dear friend, the late Dr Simon Lazar. He imparted it to me, with no special instructions except to take it from him. He did tell me the night before he took his own life that the book had undone his increasingly fragile grip on his personal reality.

Dr Lazar was a practising psychiatrist who had become disenchanted with the processes of the analytic process. He was in crisis. It is not uncommon for one who listens to the suffering of others to begin to absorb some of their pain. Some of their disease. During the turmoil of his personal despair, a woman walked into his office. She left a journal with him and never returned. Her words clearly appealed to his despair and finally, sadly, it seems the book drove Simon Lazar to take his own life.

The letter he left claimed that he had done it out of a hopeless love for Maya — the woman who had dominated his mind and dreams for a brief but pivotal period in his life.

We wish to extend gratitude to Catherine Lazar, who donated his notes from the period of time during his breakdown. We have included them as an epilogue to the *Maya 29* manuscript. They bear witness to a man who was obsessed by the words he was reading; *Maya 29* infiltrated his unconscious in a way that was ultimately destructive. It bears witness to the enduring power of the written word.

— William St. John

XXXI

Maya 29

With this pen, I am building the cemetery to lay my lovers down. These are the eulogies for all the men who fucked me into existence; for the men who fucked me out of it again. When I am done writing, I will no longer be Maya.

I will no longer be.

This is the necrology, a one-sided epistolary and the letters will be returned to the great amniotic sea with affection and fume.

The period at the end of the last sentence is the last good bullet.

Coming soon from

The Watcher and the Watched

Michael Crawley

Petra is more than a voyeur: she finds sexual gratification from her intrusion into the secret life of others. Living in a glass tower-block, she spies on opposite windows and constructs art through computer manipulation of the sexual images she steals. Then, one couple begin to intrigue and captivate her more than any previous subjects...

Realising that they are being watched, Hugh and Millie perform elaborate erotic games and Petra is soon caught in a spiral of desire and sexual excess. As the cat and mouse game accelerates, new participants from Crystal Towers are lured into the couplings, throwing Petra's cloak of anonymity into utter confusion.

How far will it go?

Coming soon from

EROS

Dark Matter

Michael Perkins

Dark Matter is the story of Robin Flood and Buddy Tate and of their collision. As they pursue their common goal of assassination, their love becomes cruel.

Set in 1999, in San Francisco's radical sexual underground where Thomas Flood is a powerful televangelist who is calling for a national crusade against evil. He urges his millions of viewers to join him in bringing his anti-pagan, anti-sex message to San Francisco on the eve of Armageddon.

Robin Flood is the televangelist's rebellious daughter: a slender, neo-pagan witch on a quest for identity. She is tattooed and pierced, transgender and transgressive, and angry because of her abused childhood. When she meets Buddy Tate, a man whose sole ambition is to get noticed any way he can, she persuades him to kill her father. In the process, she falls in love. Against the background of a war for the American soul, Robin and Buddy play out the themes of love, betrayal, death and renewal.

Coming soon from

Into the Black

David Aaron Clark

Into the Black is a highly charged tale of a beautiful woman's spiralling descent into the unseen world of supernatural predators and parasites who feed on the human race.

A traumatic, surreal brush with a mysterious force on Christmas Eve leaves Mary Ellen Masters with a stigmata and a new sense, a electric form of perception which allows her to see the New York City she grew up in as an entirely new place, a grand necropolis where the gruesome and the sublime exist a vibration away from human detection.

Already having situated herself on the fringes of society, the professional dominatrix finds herself unable to continue the life she had known, to the sadness and anger of her lovers, friends and clients. How can Mary Ellen hope to keep her body and soul intact, faced with a howling horde of seemingly immortal demons, hungry for a piece of both?

MAIL ORDER

All Eros Plus titles are available from all good bookshops or by mail order from Eros Plus Mail Order Department, 42-44 Dolben Street, London, SE1 0UP. For a free catalogue and regular updates on forth-coming titles, please enclose a large stamped SAE to the above address, quoting reference EP1-M29 on both envelopes.